Eliza & The Gnomes
Beneath
the Garden Stair

by Marie Landles

Landles Books
www.landlesbooks.com

ISBN 9781999096823

Dedicated to Kate-Anne,
who was the first to believe in me
and who loves this story.

Chapter One

Now as it was her favorite thing to do, it was not the least bit extraordinary for Eliza to be sitting outside, after everyone was fast asleep, staring at the stars and wondering. Eliza wondered about many things. Things like how many raindrops did it take to make a puddle. How many feathers did the hummingbirds, who sipped nectar from the flowers have and was it possible to teach snowflakes to build their own snowman?

It was on such a night Eliza had come out to the garden again to sit on the steps. The world was such a magical place and there were so many wonderful things to admire. Eliza was happy. Tonight, was special. Tonight, was her first night of wondering on the beautiful new back doorstep!

Her father had thought it was best if the silly old wooden stairs which had been her wondering steps, were replaced, as for some reason or other, he could never seem to keep them repaired. There was always one thing or another going wrong. There would be a loose screw laying on the rug, how it got there was anyone's guess because as far as Eliza knew, screws and bolts could not unscrew themselves to say nothing of finding their way to the old, faded rug in front of the door.

Another time, her father had replaced a badly rotting board only to come out the next morning to find the new board in almost the same state as the old. Then there was the wiggly handrail, the squeaky tread, the missing knob on the newel post and the list went on. Finally, Father had enough. It was out with the old and in with the new!

Eliza's father truly did love the old cottage they lived in, but it was his responsibility to make sure the family was safe, and a new step was a must. Much to Eliza's relief, the new step was indeed, an old step her father had found no one was using. He brought the new, old step home and it was the perfect step for their lovely old house. Eliza was so excited to try it out. She found herself wondering if her wondering would be as good on the "nold" step. Eliza could not call it a new step as it most definitely was not new, it was simply new to her and as there was not another word she could use to say that, nold would have to do.

Eliza wrapped her fuzzy pink robe around her and plunked down on the top step. She wiggled a bit looking for the most comfortable spot and scrunching her robe under her bare toes, settled in for a wonder. But the wondering did not happen. Eliza closed her eyes tight and tried awfully hard, but nope! Not a single wonder entered her head. Eliza was confused.

She never had any problem wondering before. Perhaps, it was the step.

Eliza jumped up and shook the dust from her housecoat. She skipped down the steps and stood, with her hands on her hips, considering her best course of action. This really was a lovely old step and she was sure it would be perfectly good for wondering... she only had to find her spot.

Eliza tried again. The second step this time. First on the left side, then on the right, and finally, right in the very middle. Unfortunately for Eliza, not a single wonder came to mind. Eliza was not discouraged. She scooted right down to the bottom step. Maybe she would have better luck there. Again, she tried the right side and then the left as well as the middle but again, not a single wonder. By now, Eliza was getting quite concerned. Wondering was, after all, her favorite thing to do and the back step was her favorite place to do it! There had to be a perfectly wonderful wondering spot. There simply had to be.

Eliza stood before the steps, taking a long hard look at them, trying to see if somehow, she would magically be able to see the exact spot where she should sit to wonder. She had been staring at the step for an exceedingly long time when suddenly she noticed something twinkle. Eliza looked closer. There in the next-to-last step from the bottom was a tiny handprint, not nearly as big as hers was, but about the size of the little baby next door. Written in scraggly printing beside the handprint was the name Sarah and right above the 'r' in Sarah was a sparkly stone. Eliza ran her fingers over the handprint and the letters in the name and looked intently at the stone. It was a deep, dark blue and glittered and shone in the flickering light of the streetlamp.

Eliza sat down on the step beside the handprint. The stone step here was smooth and cool against her hand, not rough as it had been on either edge of the other steps. Eliza began to wonder who Sarah was, and how her handprint came to be in the step. She wondered if perhaps Sarah had liked to sit on the step as well and perhaps that was why it was worn so smooth in that particular spot. She also wondered why the shiny blue stone was sunk into the step beside it. Suddenly, Eliza stopped! She had found her spot. She was wondering.

Eliza leaned back, her elbows resting on the step behind her and looked at the stars. She was about to begin wondering if it was possible to count them when she thought she heard a tiny …. sniff. Eliza stayed absolutely still and listened. She began to wonder if she was hearing things when she heard the sound again.

"Sniff, sniff"

It sounded to Eliza like someone, someone exceedingly small, was… crying!

Now Eliza was a kind little girl. Even at the ripe old age of 6 and ¾ and 2 days, she knew if someone was crying, she should try her best to help.

Eliza was forever rescuing ladybugs who managed to find their way inside their lovely old stone house. She had often wondered if they accidentally came inside because they had mistaken the flowers on her dresses as real flowers. Eliza was very fond of flowers and therefore, had flowers on almost every garment she wore, including her lovely little shoes. It would be quite easy for a little ladybug to think they were real flowers. In fact, Eliza had wondered how they might be able to tell the difference at all.

It was also widely known about the neighborhood, Eliza was one for rescuing caterpillars from the hot cement sidewalks, small toads from puddles which were about to dry up and even on occasion, a kitten who after very kitten-ish hi-jinx would end up in all manner of difficulties, but that's another story.

Suffice to say, Eliza had a reputation for being kind.

"Sniff"

Eliza hunkered down, her chin on her knees as she listened intently to see if she could determine where, exactly, the sniffling was coming from. She turned her head a little to the right.

"Sniff…sniff"

Then she turned her head to the left.

"Sniff"

Yes, it was definitely louder, on the left. Eliza peeked through the rails on the step, trying to see if the sniffing was coming somewhere from the vicinity of the garden next to the step. The garden was full of bright flowers, now mostly closed and sleeping, as were most of the creatures in the garden.

"Sniff"

Eliza wiggled even closer to the railing and squinted her eyes, wondering if it would help her see better, but it was too dark to make out anything other than the nodding heads of the peony bush.

"Sniff"

Quick as can be, Eliza scooched down the steps and getting down on her hands and knees, peered under the bushy leaves of the 4 O'clocks. 4 O'clocks were one of the few flowers which stayed open all night as they did not open until the late afternoon. Their sweet fragrance drifted over the garden like mist.

"Sniff… sniff"

Eliza knew the sniffing was definitely coming from this part of the garden, but it was still far too dark for her to see anything.

Scrambling to her feet she quietly slipped up the stairs and through the back door. Eliza needed something to help her see and Father always kept a small flashlight in the kitchen drawer, next to the pantry, she was allowed to use. It was not a big flashlight like his. It was a tiny, little flashlight shaped like a worm. A funny, little round green worm exactly the right size for her 6 and ¾ and 2 days size hands.

Slipping quietly back out into the garden, Eliza laid down on the grass so she could shine her little worm light under the leaves. First, she shone the light to the left... nothing. Then she shone her little light to the right…hmm. Nothing there either. Eliza wondered if she was imagining.

"Sniff… "

Eliza shone the light in the direction of the sniff. At first, she could not see anything, but then, as she was about to look away, she saw it. The tiny toe of a …. a shoe, peeking out from under the broad leaf of a Hosta plant. What on earth would a shoe be doing there, Eliza wondered. More importantly, who's shoe? Eliza inched forward to get a better look, all the while trying not to frighten whom-ever belonged to the tiny little shoe. The little shoe was not like any shoe Eliza had seen before. It did not seem much like a shoe really, at least not the kind of shoes she was familiar with. This little shoe was more like a slipper, but it seemed to be made of moss. Curious indeed!

"Sniff…. sniff"

It must have been quite a sight for the old owl who lived

in the big elm tree in the garden to see. Eliza on all fours, her bum up and her head buried amidst the flowers and ferns of the flower bed, holding tightly to her little, green worm light, her toes peeking out from under her bright, pink, fuzzy housecoat.

Trying to find the source of the sniffs and the owner of the little moss shoe kept Eliza far to busy to pay any attention to the owl. She edged a little closer. She did not dare get too close because she knew there were sometimes skunks and hedgehogs in the garden, and she did not want to surprise one of those. Eliza grinned and chuckled to herself. Silly girl, hedgehogs do not wear shoes!

Eliza got as close as she dared. Then slowly, she picked up the very tippy tip of a Hosta leaf and shone her little worm light beneath it. There, in the dark, with only the slight glow of Eliza's little light, was a tiny little …. gnome.

The idea there might be gnomes in the garden was something Eliza had long suspected. In fact, she had rather hoped there were! Eliza loved to wonder about gnomes and fairies and the like and often imagined what it would be like should she ever have the privilege of meeting them. This little fellow was not what Eliza had expected. But then, come to think of it, it was quite possible Eliza really had not known what to expect! Regardless, there before her very eyes, was, apparently …a gnome.

The little fellow, or she assumed he was a he, was huddled back against the wall of the house. He was in his entirety, about the size of one of Mother's teacups. He wore a tall, pointy hat of dark green, the same dark green as his coat. The wide rim came down and rested on the bridge of his nose obscuring his eyes. Its point was shaped like a fishhook and at the very tip of it was a tiny bell. His nose was jolly and plump, and his white whiskers formed a long flowing beard. He wore a loose-

Gus

11

fitting coat with wide, flared sleeves. His hands were tucked beneath his beard and with his coat, long, all Eliza could see, were his tiny shoes peeking out from under the hem.

All the garden gnomes Eliza had ever seen had been merely statues. They all looked the same with their tall straight red caps, white beards and silly shirts which all seemed to be two sizes too small. They always appeared to be up to mischief. Eliza much preferred this little gnome.

The little gnome appeared to belong in Eliza's garden. Eliza wiggled a bit closer.

"That's quite close enough if you please!" exclaimed the gnome. His voice was incredibly low, and it surprised her a little man… gnome… gnome-man, would have such a deep, husky voice.

Startled, Eliza froze where she was.

"OH!" she exclaimed, "You talk!"

"Well of course I talk," huffed the gnome. He seemed to puff himself up as to make himself appear bigger, much like Eliza had seen the baby robins do when her dog Twiggles had gotten too close.

"Well" whispered Eliza, "I think it is exceptionally clever of you!"

The little gnome rustled his coat and seemed to puff up slightly more. Eliza thought she should perhaps say something to put the little fellow at ease.

"My name is Eliza Fitch" said Eliza. "This is my house and my garden, and I am very pleased to meet you."

The little gnome de-puffed slightly.

"And what pray-tell is your name?" Eliza inquired. The little man did not respond.

"Oh, I see," she said. "Perhaps you don't have a name, is that it?" The little man puffed up even more. There was a great ruffling and rustling as the little man, clearly annoyed, stomped a teeny bit closer to Eliza.

"Of course, I have a name, silly goose! Everything has a name so why shouldn't I have a name!" he blustered.

Eliza was about to say something else and ask his name again when the little man stomped right up to her. Sticking out his fat little hand, and patting Eliza right on the end of her nose he announced,

"my moniker is Fratternagle Oferious Stout". Eliza blinked. "But" he continued, "most people call me Gus".

"How do you do Mr. Gus" said Eliza, her voice hushed and quiet. (She had always been taught to address people by Mr. or Mrs. She considered it to be completely appropriate) "it is lovely to make your acquaintance." Eliza wasn't exactly sure what such a big word as acquaintance meant, but she had heard her mother say it many times when the ladies had come for tea, so she felt it would be alright if she was to use it this time.

"Not MR. Gus you Ninny" huffed the little man. "Just Gus, plain Gus".

"Oh!" said Eliza, "I am deeply sorry… Gus".

Eliza stared at Gus, and Gus stood there staring at Eliza. Eliza was wondering what she should do next when it occurred to her perhaps, she should sit up.

"Gus," Eliza said, "would you mind terribly if I was to sit up? Perhaps, with your permission, we could even retire to the steps to continue our conversation? I would very much like to get to know you better."

Gus pondered her request. "I think," he said, "that is a very cordial idea providing…nothing up there wants to eat me!"

Eliza gasped "good heavens!! Why would anything want to eat you!"

"Shows what you know! Don't you know anything bigger than me usually wants to invite me for dinner… AS DINNER!"

Eliza was horrified! Surely, Gus must be mistaken. She did not know him well, but it still seemed highly unreasonable anything would want to eat him. It did seem, at that moment, the first thing she needed to do was to reassure him he would not, in fact, be eaten.

"Gus," she said simply, "I give you my word, as your friend and your protector, you will definitely and most decidedly NOT be eaten."

Eliza let go of the leaf and slowly started to wiggle her way out of the flower bed with Gus hesitantly following. Finally, Eliza was able to sit up and taking a moment to pluck the odd blossom and leaf from her hair, waited for Gus to catch up.

Gus nervously peered out from the safety of the foliage and took a couple of timid steps toward Eliza. She looked ever so much bigger sitting up than she had when they had first met. Mind you, he had only been able to see her face, but it was significantly larger than his own so it would only stand to reason, the rest of her was significantly bigger as well.

It became obvious to Eliza, Gus was more than a little bit frightened and she could not help but wonder what it must be like to suddenly meet someone so unexpectantly.

"Gus," she said, "I give you my word. Everything will be fine and if you like, you may ride on my hand and I will carry you up onto the step where we can have a chat."

Placing her hand, palm side up on the cool soil, she waited for Gus to make his decision. Slowly, and then with perhaps a bit more courage, Gus stepped forward and then climbed into Eliza's waiting palm. Eliza lifted him up gently and turned to sit on the step.

"Slow down!" exclaimed Gus "I won't have to worry about being eaten if I fall to my death!"

Eliza stopped cold. It had not occurred to her any movement she made, no matter how small, would be like speeding down the lane in Father's car for Gus.

"I am sorry Gus… I forgot."

Cupping her hand around Gus, as you would to keep a candle from blowing out as you walked, Eliza moved slowly to the wondering step and sat down, placing her hand on her knee so Gus could jump out.

"Now," said Eliza, "perhaps you can tell me why you were crying?"

Gus bent over and smoothed some of the fluff of Eliza's housecoat down and took a seat. Taking a deep breath, Gus began to tell her his story.

Chapter Two

"It's really quite simple" Gus explained. "I can't get home."

"Home?" Eliza asked, "what do you mean you can't get home. Isn't the garden your home?"

Gus sighed, and Eliza heard a small "sniff".

"No" Gus's voice had a quiver to it. "my family has tended this garden for hundreds of years and we love it here, but our home…. is under the stairs." Gus's voice trailed off and Eliza blinked two or three times as she began to understand. Their home was under the stairs? The old stairs? The stairs her father had replaced!

"OH MY! Gus, whatever shall you do?" Eliza exclaimed! Then, as she began to think about it more… "Gus! You said your family! Is there more like you? Living here? Under these stairs?"

Gus raised his hands to calm Eliza down. She was getting quite excited and Gus was afraid she would forget how small he was, and it made him nervous.

"Yes, my family all live here. I am sure they are quite safe; our home is underground. Today, I was out tending the snails in the moss field. When I came home, the old step was gone, and this new step was here." Gus sniffed, then carried on.

"We don't have a door in this new step. We have no way to come and go from our home and there is ever so much work to do. I will never be able to do it all alone."

Eliza listened intently. She could hardly believe what she was hearing. Not only was there a gnome living in the garden, but there was an entire family of gnomes. She waited for Gus to go on.

"It has always been our job to look after all the tiniest creatures who live in the garden. We look after polishing the ladybug shells, they have impossibly short legs you know." Eliza nodded.

"We train grasshoppers and bumblebees for the fairy trade." Eliza's eyes lit up, but she said nothing, there would be time for questions later. "We take down the used spider webs and wind up the silk to weave for our clothes and most importantly, we help all the flowers open every morning."

"ALL of them?" Eliza whispered in awe, glancing around at the flower beds lining the garden.

"All of them" replied Gus, nodding his head matter of factly.

"There must be a great many people in your family?" Eliza said in wonder. "There are ever so many flowers in our garden".

Gus shrugged his shoulders and fluffed up his beard. "Well, not really," he said, "there is Fitzhenry Terwilligar Popillary Jones, we call him Fritz, he's away visiting the old country. Onshonery Standopoulous Bent… that's Toad. Then there is Hagidaar Methodius Dewellen Vempompery Snip, he's known as Snip and my wife, Constantina Sambrigidan Pipps… that's my Jenny. Oh, I almost forgot…and Sebastian."

Eliza smiled at the wonderful names. "Gus" she said, "why are all your names so…long and so funny? They almost sound like songs."

"It's quite simple. We gnomes live for an exceptionally long

18

time, so we only celebrate our birthday's every 100 years. Each birthday, as a present, we are given another name." Gus explained.

"My goodness, Gus! That means you are 300 years old"

Gus blushed and began twisting his beard between his hands. "Jenny and me" he gushed, "are newlyweds!" Eliza giggled.

It was at that very moment, a light blinked on in the house. Gus dove for cover down the sleeve of Eliza's fuzzy robe. Eliza giggled again. Gus tickled! She heard the window in her parent's room open and Father's voice seemed loud in the quiet of the garden.

"Eliza, it's well past your bedtime! Time you came in!" her father did not sound as if he was teasing so she answered.

"Yes, Father. I will, right away." The window shut and the light went out.

Gus peeked out of his hiding place and clambered onto the step beside her.

"You heard my Father" whispered Eliza "we must go in. Jump into my pocket and you can spend the night in my room. Then, in the morning, we can see what needs to be done."

"Go in! I cannot go in your house. The cat will get me!"

Gus had begun to jump up and down in hysterics. Eliza tried her best not to laugh, he looked silly, but she could tell he was terribly upset.

"First of all, Gus, we don't have a cat and our dog will be sound asleep on his cushion beside the hearth. I have a lovely dollhouse which will do quite well for you for tonight. We cannot leave you out here it looks like it might rain."

Gus was not listening. He was still stomping and huffing back and forth along the step. His arms would occasionally flutter wildly as he seemed to be imagining all sorts of things which might go wrong if he should go into the house with her.

Finally, Eliza simply scooped Gus up and gently depositing him into her pocket. Picking up her little worm flashlight she went in-doors and up the stairs to her room.

It was a bit of a bumpy ride for Gus, who was trapped in her pocket, as he thumped and bumped against her leg with each step up the stairs, but finally, they reached the top. Eliza went into the bathroom and washed her face and hands and brushed her teeth. She found a small cup and filled it with lovely, warm water and took it with her into her room. She had no idea if gnomes bathed, but in case, she felt she would not be a proper host if she did not at least offer Gus a chance to clean up, after his long day working in her garden.

She gently closed the door to her room and walked over to the low table on which sat a beautiful, almost identical small house which matched her wonderful, old house she lived in. Her father had built her this lovely house for her dolls and although Eliza had quite a few dolls, she had always felt this house was more for fairies than dolls. She had never imagined it would have a gnome for a guest.

Eliza carefully opened the quaint little house and poured

the cup full of water into the bathtub. There was a drop or two still clinging to the rim of the cup and she dripped them into the basin. She could feel Gus squirming inside her pocket, but she did not want to let him out until everything was perfect. In the tall cupboard in her room, next to the toy box, Eliza took out a large box. Inside the box was all the doll clothes and accessories for her house and she went to work laying out the tiniest towels imaginable as well as a rug, slippers, and a robe. She wasn't at all sure what gnomes ate for dinner, but as always, Mother had left her a snack on the table beside her bed and she broke off a bit of cheese, broke a cracker into 4 small pieces and added a raspberry, then filled a tiny cup with milk and set the whole thing on the tiny kitchen table. When she was finished, she stood back and nodding her approval, scooped Gus out of her pocket and set him on the table in front of the door.

Gus was slightly ruffled by his trip up the stairs but was none the worse for wear, except perhaps for his temper. He was about to start to stomp and bluster again. He shook his coat and smoothed his beard and stroked his hat trying to smooth out the small dents, then turned to shake his head and his finger at Eliza.

"What do you mean to do bashing me all about! Look what you did to my hat... what in the blue blazes ...." Gus's voice faded to nothing as he turned. It was then he saw the house.

So astonished was Gus at the sight of the miniature cottage so familiar to him, all he could do was huff!

"Goodness me!"

"Will it do? Gus, do you think this will be alright? You will be perfectly safe here." Eliza was most concerned that Gus might not like to be staying in a doll's house, but she had nowhere else to put him. Gus wasn't saying anything. He was standing and staring at the little house. Finally, after what seemed like a very long time to Eliza, Gus began to speak. His voice was quiet and soft.

"You want me…to stay here?"

"Well, yes, actually. Oh Gus, I tried to make it most inviting. There is a lovely little supper for you, and I put warm water in the bathtub, and I managed to find a clean robe and some slippers." Eliza was talking so fast; Gus could hardly keep up.

Gus raised his hand to stem the flow of words.

"Eliza," he said softly "this is the most beautiful house I have ever seen. It would be my privilege to stay here, but it all seems much too much. I have only seen houses like this on the cover of Better Gnomes and Gardens!"

Eliza smiled. "Thank you, Gus. It is quite lovely, but I have not used it much. My dolls do not seem to belong in it, and I did not really realize it until I saw you standing in front of it! This is a house for gnomes, not dolls." Gus shook his head.

"No Eliza," he said. "Gnomes do not live in houses like this. We like our homes underground where it is peaceful and quiet and dark." Eliza sighed. Gus quickly continued "but fairies would love this house! Of course, they would redecorate… they use flower petals for everything, lampshades, bed coverings, curtains… that sort of thing. Yes, I think fairies would like this house very much!" Eliza grinned and softly clapped her hands.

"Oh, Gus! Do you really think so? Do you happen to know some fairies? Oh, I have always wanted to meet fairies!"

Gus did in fact, know quite a few fairies and Eliza was delighted. He was about to tell her all about his fairy friends when he saw her yawn and slowly rub her eyes. It was getting late. Gus yawned too.

"Thank you for rescuing me Eliza," Gus said softly, "I still do not know what I am going to do, but it helps to have a safe place to sleep tonight… and a new, very nice, young friend.

If it is all right with you, I would very much like to go to bed now. It has been a long day and a very upsetting one at that."

Eliza nodded. "Of course, Gus!" she said, "go on into the house. I think you will find everything in order. I will close it once you have gone in so you might have some privacy. Good Night."

Waiting until Gus had found his way up the steps and into the house, Eliza carefully closed the two halves together. She flicked the little switch for the night light. She did not need a night light anymore, but she thought it might give enough light for Gus so he might have some comfort in such a strange place.

Pulling back the coverlet, Eliza shrugged out of her bright pink, fuzzy robe and tossed it onto the chair beside the bed. Then, she slipped into bed pulling the covers up under her chin. She grinned to herself as she listened to her new friend Gus, munching on the supper she had left out for him. It sounded a bit like the time they had a mouse in the cupboard. Eliza yawned and snuggled deeper into her bed. There was the soft rumble of thunder far away and Eliza was very thankful Gus was safe and warm and dry inside. It did appear it would rain tonight. She smiled again as she started to drift off to sleep with the sound of Gus splashing in the bathtub. It seemed, gnomes, did bathe after all.

Chapter Three

The next morning, Eliza woke to the sound of raindrops hitting her window. Peering out, under the lace curtain, she saw it was very wet indeed. There were puddles all along the path out in the garden. Rivulets of water streamed down her windowpane and all the flowers in the garden were bent over with the weight of the rain. It was, as the adults would say, a lovely, good rain. The clouds in the sky were heavy and low and from all appearances, were settled in for a steady day's rain. Eliza sighed. She did not mind the rain. Everything always smelled so fresh and lovely afterward and she did love to watch the raindrops, sliding down the windows. It would mean though, she might not have a chance to spend as much time out in the garden as usual. Then, of course, there was Gus. GUS!!!

Eliza whirled around and peeked at the dollhouse. Everything seemed quiet. She quietly opened her closet and pulled a cozy sweater and pants from the shelves. Adding some fuzzy socks to the pile in her arms, and digging her slippers out from under the bed, Eliza slipped out to the bathroom to dress.

After she had washed her hands and face, brushed her teeth and gotten dressed, Mother, gently brushed her hair, and put in her pigtails. Eliza had always heard how she had hair like her Grandmother's, but Eliza could never understand. Her Grandmother's hair was white! Eliza's hair was a golden red/brown particularly red in the sunshine. It was more wavy than curly but curly enough her Mother preferred it in pigtails as it was not quite so difficult to brush it out. It was long enough Eliza could barely catch it in her fingertips if she bent her head back and reached behind her back. Eliza often wondered how fairies managed to brush their hair. All the pictures she had seen of fairies, and there were quite a few, all showed fairies to have lovely long hair. How in the world would a fairy brush it … especially after flying all about?

All finished, Eliza skipped down the hall to her room and hung up her nightgown. She made her bed and was fluffing the pillow when she heard a gruff voice behind her.

"Good morning Eliza," Gus said.

"Good morning to you as well Gus. I hope you slept well?" Gus nodded and Eliza dropped down to her knees in front of the table where the little house sat, looking at Gus peering out of the window.

"Um, would you mind, I mean, if it's convenient for you, to…. Let ME OUT!!" Gus apparently, was NOT a morning person.

Eliza gasped, but quickly opened the two halves of the house so it spread apart. Out stomped Gus seemingly quite perturbed about something, Eliza grinned, perhaps, she should make it perturbed about everything!

"It's about time!" Gus blustered, "what in the devil took so long!! I could have added another name in that amount of time!"

Stifling a giggle, Eliza immediately apologized. "I'm sorry Gus. I thought you might still be sleeping so I didn't rush."

"Sleeping! At this hour! When there is so much to do!! Not on my Aunt Thimbles garter straps!"

Oh my, thought Eliza. Gus was a very grumpy gnome!

"Gus," Eliza said softly, a giggle lurking below the surface, "don't fret so! It is still early and as it is pouring rain you won't need to open any of the flowers!" Gus seemed to be even more flustered by her words.

"Rain! Did you say rain? Pouring, yes that is the word you used, pouring rain! Oh my! Oh Dear!! Goodness me! Oh fiddlesticks!" Gus was really agitated now and was pacing wildly, back, and forth, along the edge of the table. So close in fact, that Eliza feared he might fall off.

"Calm yourself, Gus! You must calm down. If you are not careful you could fall off the table. Please calm down. I will help you!" Gus did not hear her. He was too busy stomping up and down, first one way then he would whirl about and march right back in the direction he had come from. Eliza watched him for a moment or two and then realizing nothing good was going to come from him getting more and more upset, decided to take some action. Gus looked so silly stomping up and down, and Eliza was trying so hard not to laugh, tears were beginning to form and threatened to give her merriment away by sliding conspicuously down her cheeks.

Carefully, to avoid actually hitting him and knocking him off the table, Eliza reached out and caught the tail of his coat, as it dragged a smidgeon behind him, with one finger, pinning it to the table. Gus did not notice, and he kept tromping along, arms swinging, muttering under his beard until he finally realized he wasn't going anywhere.

Gus looked over his shoulder, first at Eliza, her eyes sparkling with laughter, then gradually looking down her long arm to where her finger was pinning his cloak to the table. With a huff, Gus simply plunked down, his arms folded across his chest, his back to her.

"Now Gus. Don't be cross! You really must calm down." Eliza used her softest, gentlest voice, trying hard not to let him see her laugh.

"Bumsknuckles!" was Gus's stern reply.

That did it, Eliza could not hold it in anymore and she fell over, on the floor, not only giggling but full out laughing. Gus was NOT amused.

Eliza giggled until her sides began to hurt, then she sat up, cross-legged on the rug, wiping the tears streaming down her cheeks away with the back of her hand.

"OH! Gus, I am sorry! You looked so funny!"

"FROG WADDLES" shouted Gus. Eliza collapsed.

After what seemed like an exceedingly long time to Gus, Eliza finally stopped laughing. She lay on the floor and turning her head, looked up at the table and her new friend. Gus was sitting with his legs hanging over the table edge, staring down at her. Eliza could not see his eyes, but she could tell from his posture, that he was indeed scowling at her.

"Are you quite finished?" grumbled Gus.

"Yes," said Eliza contritely, "quite."

"This is no laughing matter you know! It will be pandemonium out in the garden!" Gus was still frantic. Eliza realized Gus was earnestly upset, and apparently, for good reason. She immediately sat up and decided to be serious.

"What do you mean Gus. It is raining. The flowers never open when it rains so what is it that you must do?"

"What must I do?" Gus was almost shouting. "Everything!! I must do everything! There is no one to help me... remember... no door!"

The little gnome's words brought Eliza back to reality. She had almost forgotten. Gus's entire family helped him tend the garden, and although she had no idea what all the jobs were, they had to do, there was obviously a great deal to be done and only Gus to do it.

"I'll help you, Gus. Let me help you!"

Gus looked at her skeptically.

"Please, Gus? Please let me help."

Gus really did not have much choice.

"Do you have a writing stick and paper Eliza?" Gus asked.

Eliza scrambled to the desk and took out a piece of paper and a purple crayon.

"Write this down" instructed Gus.

"I don't know how to write that good, I am just learning my letters" whispered a sad Eliza.

"OH! HOBNOBBERS!" exclaimed Gus.

"GUS!" exclaimed Eliza.

Gus had begun to stomp away, but he stopped and looked back over his shoulder at Eliza. He could tell that she really was trying to help. He did not have a clue as to what she might be able to do, her being a human and a giant and all, but it seemed he had no choice. Turning back, he walked into the house and pulled out a small chair. Eliza sat closer and rested her chin on the table.

"Tell me" she requested.

"Have you ever milked a June bug?" Gus asked.

"No" replied Eliza.

"Didn't think you had" sighed Gus shaking his head.

"How about harness a grasshopper?"

"Nope"

"Sailed a sweet pea pod canoe?"

"No"

Gus continued to ask Eliza a multitude of questions. Eliza, unfortunately, had to continue to answer no to each and every one. She had no idea how many jobs there were to be done. She spent a great deal of time in the garden and she had never noticed Gus or any of his family doing any of the jobs he was talking about. Milk a June bug! Whoever heard of such a thing.

Gus went on down his list of things absolutely needing to be done. Eliza answered no to each and every one until Gus happened to say, "know how to build a door?"

"YES!" she shouted, sending Gus tumbling wildly head over heels out of his chair until he landed, feet up, flat on his back, looking up, against the wall of the little house. "oops, sorry, I forgot. Well, I don't exactly know how to build a door, but I know someone who does!"

Gus clamoured to his feet with a little help from Eliza and shuffled his cloak back into place.

"Well," he said, "I guess we better start there then. I will need help to do the rest, and you won't do. We best figure out how we can get the others out. The earthworms will have to figure out their own traffic jam this one time, but I am sure we will be hearing from their union." Gus shook his head and putting his hands behind his back, began to walk in a rather large circle, thinking.

Eliza had some thinking to do also. Earthworms? Traffic jam? Union? Goodness, she was certainly going to have some incredibly different things to wonder about after this!

Gus finally stopped pacing and picking up his chair, sat down again, a little safer distance from Eliza than the last time.

"Now," he said, "about the door."

As Gus had already determined building a door was going to be the first priority, Eliza carefully began to explain what she knew about door building to Gus.

"You see, next door to us is our neighbor. He is a genuinely nice old man and he is my friend. His name is Mr. McGuigan. Father says Mr. McGuigan used to be a carpenter and I bet he has built ever so many doors. He once built a birdhouse for me for in the garden and it has been full of birds ever since! It did not have a door, but that does not matter. Birdhouses never have doors. I am sure we can ask for his help, but first, … breakfast!"

Eliza was about to head out of her door when she stopped. "Oh dear, I will need to find someplace to hide you and still be able to carry you about. My sweater doesn't have a pocket."

"That's quite all right," said Gus, "I don't care for riding in pockets."

Looking around her room, Eliza rejected one thing after the other as suitable transportation for Gus. Finally, Eliza spied something which might be perfect. Sitting on her dressing table was a lovely little handbag. The bottom was flat, the sides were straight, fairly tall and made of something quite hard, so they stood up straight. It looked a bit like a hatbox only smaller and had a lovely, flowered fabric gathered all together with a silky drawstring to make loops which became the handle. It might do very nicely. Gus would have plenty of room and anytime she needed to talk to him, she simply opened the strings. She could easily carry it about as that is what it is for, and no one would suspect a thing. It would also help that, as well as wondering, Eliza loved dress-up. No one would think anything of her wearing a raincoat and galoshes and carrying a handbag. She grinned to herself, being 6 and ¾ and 3 days was such fun.

Eliza went to work making the handbag safe for Gus. She added a small, soft, scarf to protect Gus from being tumbled about and a pair of folded socks so he might have somewhere to sit. Into the handbag, she also put another of the tiny towels from the box in the closet in case it sprung a leak. Hmmm, right. It was raining and the little fabric handbag would not take long to get soaked. That would never do. Again, Eliza needed to find a solution. She searched her room again. AHA! Perfect. Her fuzzy slippers had come in a wonderful clear plastic package with a handle. Eliza had liked it so much she had filled it with her hair ribbons. She dumped the ribbons out on her bed and set about putting the handbag, inside the plastic package. It fit! Turning, she showed it to Gus. Gus nodded his approval and Eliza lifted him from the table to her bed, then from her bed into the handbag and her handbag into the package.

"Um, Eliza?"

"Yes Gus"

"Do you think you might have a pole about?"

"A pole? What kind of pole? Whatever for?"

"Well for this handbag of course!" Gus was beginning to bluster again. "The fool thing keeps falling in on me"

Carefully examining the handbag, Eliza could definitely see there was a problem. When she used the strings of the handbag as a handle, it kept the gathers at the top stretched far away from the bottom. When the handbag was inside the plastic package, she did not use the strings for the handle, so the top collapsed into the bottom. What to do?

Another search of her room produced a small funnel from her art table. Mother had given her the funnel so she could pour some coloured sand into a pretty glass bottle Mrs.

McGuigan had given her. It might do very nicely.

Lifting Gus out, Eliza went to work. The funnel, as it happened, fit perfectly inside the rim of the walls of the handbag. The fabric would then close over it, disguising it completely, but the stem of the funnel would then protrude enough it might act as a small window so Gus would perhaps have a little bit of light. Splendid!

And down to breakfast, they went!

Chapter Four

Eliza climbed onto her chair at the breakfast table and placed the plastic case close to her foot beside her chair. She wanted to be able to keep an eye on it. She had opened the gathers at the top ever so slightly and had moved the funnel a bit, so it was relatively easy for her to drop the odd tidbit of breakfast down for Gus. First went a couple of blueberries – without the yogurt. Then a piece of cinnamon scone and a bit of cheese.

Twiggles had started to take an interest in her handbag and she had, at one point, given him a strong push away with her leg. After her promise to Gus he would not be eaten, she had to make very sure, he was not. Twiggles was a good dog, but how on earth was he to know Gus was, well, Gus, and was not perhaps a mouse or some other creature.

"Eliza, you are being quiet this morning. Is everything all right?" Eliza had jumped when her father said her name. She had been wondering, which she seldom did at the table, about how to go about building the door.

"Yes, Father" she replied, "I am perfectly fine. I was doing some wondering."

"Well, what on earth could you be wondering about all

ready on this soggy morning?"

"Oh, I was wondering how, if it were really important, one might go about making a door."

"A door Eliza? Good heavens. How odd. What kind of door dear?" asked her Mother.

"Oh, a regular door. Well, perhaps not very regular. I was wondering about building a gnome door, you know, so they could get to their house."

Father chuckled. "I see. Well, if I was wondering about doing something like that, I think perhaps I might have a chat with Mr. McGuigan. I am sure if anyone might have an idea about building such a door, it might be him." Father smiled over his cup to Mother and gave her a quick wink.

Mother smiled back and nodded. "I will give Mrs. McGuigan a quick ring and see if Mr. McGuigan might be out in his workshop. Be sure you are back in time for lunch."

"Oh yes, Mother, I will. Thank you so very much and thank you for breakfast." Eliza cleared her plate and bowl from the table and put them in the sink, then skipped to the entry to put on her raincoat and galoshes. Eliza much preferred the word galoshes to gumboots. Her mother had read her the word in a story and Eliza had called her boots, galoshes, from then on. Ga-losshhhh-es… it even sounds like splashing in a puddle.

Eliza pulled on her rain cap and pulled the elastic firmly under her chin. As much as she loved the rain, she definitely did not love drips. Drips that hit her nose and drips which ran down the back of her neck were the worst. She despised drips so much and would often make such a fuss about them, her mother had bought her a lovely wide-rimmed rain hat. The hat was a bit too big, but it worked astonishingly well for stopping all the drips, provided of course she remembered to make sure the rim of the bright yellow rain hat was outside the collar of her bright purple, flowered raincoat.

"Don't forget your handbag, Eliza," called her father from the dining room. Eliza stopped dead in her tracks! The handbag!! Poor Gus! She dashed into the other room as Twiggles was about to take a giant sniff into her bag.

"Twiggles!" she squealed "bad dog!"

"Now, now Eliza. He was not hurting anything. He was only taking a sniff. Whatcha got hidden in your handbag, anything good for him to eat?" Father was teasing she knew, but still, goodness! That was a close one!

She carefully, scooped up her bag trying her best not to jostle its inhabitant to much and quickly made her way back to the door. Twiggles was still extremely interested in her bag and followed her closely, wagging his big, bushy tail the whole way.

"Get away you big oof!" Eliza said crossly. "Get away!"

Eliza managed to get the door open without giving Twiggles a chance to get a better sniff, then headed out into the rain. Twiggles did not like to be wet, so he gave up sniffing in favour of going back to his big cushion by the hearth. It had to be a big cushion, after all, Twiggles was a sheepdog. He looked much bigger than he was because he was extraordinarily fluffy. Eliza had seen him wet when they took him to the groomers. No, it was much better if he stayed on his cushion and stayed dry. He took forever to dry out!

Walking as quickly as she dared, Eliza half-ran, and half walked down the garden path to the little shed her Father had made. Mother had not approved of his plan for a treehouse, although Eliza had thought it would be delightful, so he had made her this little shed instead. It had dark green shutters but there was no glass in the windows. The little house was painted white and Mother had printed Eliza's name over the yellow door. She had also painted flowers of every shape, size, and colour on the outside walls and it blended so perfectly into the garden, unless you knew exactly where to look, there was a very good chance you wouldn't even notice it was there. It was also her secret passage to Mr. McGuigan's garden.

When her father had first put up the shed, there had been an old gate right against the back wall. Mr. McGuigan and her father had then taken down the old gate and put in a double swing door which could open from either side. Mother and Mrs. McGuigan had approved, this way, Eliza could easily go back and forth between them and never set foot on the front sidewalk. Anyone who happened along, would never be able to see there was a passageway between the two gardens and Eliza could come and go as she pleased.

Eliza stepped quickly inside and closed the door. She could hear some scuffling coming from the corner behind the wooden crate she used as a bookshelf and the old corn broom her mother had given her to sweep out the leaves. She took no heed of it, as it was often, she found the odd mouse or mole or even a bunny seeking shelter from the rain. Closing the door behind her, she pulled a little milk stool over to the table and sat down, carefully placing the handbag on the tabletop. Gingerly, she opened the top and pulled out the funnel. She sighed with relief as she saw Gus was no worse for wear. His temper, it appeared, had not improved.

"PLUM BUFFER HOPS"

he stormed! "That great beast almost got me! Some protector you are! Where in the name of petrified wood are we now?"

"I know, I'm sorry, and he's not a great beast, he's only a dog. He didn't mean any harm he was merely sniffing." It was understandable to Gus, Twiggles might have seemed extraordinarily big indeed. There was no point arguing with Gus about it. He was already as mad as a wet hen. May as well change the subject.

"This is my shed, Gus. This is the way to Mr. McGuigan's garden. But first, we need to come up with a plan. I can't ask Mr. McGuigan to build something I know nothing about. He will ask me all sorts of questions and I don't know anything about how a gnome door should be."

There was more rustling in the corner.

"Do you still have that paper and your writing stick?" asked Gus.

"No," said Eliza. "But! I think I have some here!" Quickly Eliza went over to the shelf on the wall where she kept a lovely, long metal tin. The tin had been given to her by her Grandmother. She had used it to keep animal crackers inside for Eliza, which were her favorite. When her Grandmother had moved out of her house, and no longer needed the tin, she had gifted it to Eliza as she knew how much Eliza had loved it. The tin was green and silver with a very delicate pattern and even though it was ever so old and some of the paint was a bit faded, it still meant the world to Eliza. She may not have her Grandmother anymore, but she had Grandmother's biscuit tin.

Inside the tin, was some rolled-up sheets of paper, a few bits of crayon and sidewalk chalk, some coloured string, a couple of sparkly, very flat stones, two coloured paperclips, a brass button, an empty wooden thread spool, a small knitting needle, a feather, a shiny gold thimble and a lovely red bead.

Eliza was in the habit of keeping all sorts of bits and bobs. She had tins and boxes filled with treasures and would spend many a rainy day out in the shed simply looking at them. She only kept the really special things in Grandmother's old biscuit tin.

Eliza carried the tin to the table. Carefully she lifted out the paper and smoothed it out. She had to lift it out very carefully because the moment she had set the tin on the table, Gus had shuffled over to it and was snooping about, his nose right over the rim of the tin and was bouncing ever so slightly in excitement! It appeared gnomes had an eye for treasure too.

"Now," said Eliza very matter of fact-ly, "about this door."

Gus pulled himself away from the treasures in the tin and came over and plunked down, crossing his feet beneath him, on the corner of the paper, resting his chin, or what appeared to be his chin under all those whiskers, on his hand and his elbow on his knee. He appeared to be thinking.

"Well," Gus muttered, "I suppose the very first thing we must do is decide where to put it". Goodness, Eliza had not thought of that. Where would they put it? It would not be possible to put a door in the stone step, that was quite ridiculous. Father would likely not approve of them putting a hole in their little old house either. Hmmm, it was a problem.

"Gus, what sorts of places are good for doors?" Eliza asked.

"I seem to recollect..." Eliza raised one eyebrow questionably.

"it means remember" answered Gus. Clearing his throat, he continued. "I seem to remember,

40

there was once a door, under the step of the hand pump over by the raspberry patch." He seemed to be deep in thought, so Eliza did not interrupt. "but that was years ago. I only had two names then."

"We don't have a pump by the raspberry patch Gus," said Eliza softly.

More rustling came from the corner, as well as, what Eliza could only describe, as a muffled, huff!

"Then, of course, there was one on the side of the old out-house." Gus shook his head "I was barely a boy then" he mumbled.

Eliza giggled. The corner rustled more, and Eliza was sure she saw the broomstick wiggle. She was becoming suspicious.

"My favorite" continued Gus, unaware that Eliza was now keeping one eye on the corner and the broomstick while focusing the rest of her attention on him, "was definitely the one in the woodshed. It was such a lovely door and had the most charming front step..." his voice trailed off wistfully.

The broom shattered the silence by banging down onto the floor. Eliza jumped and Gus puffed up like a fat little partridge.

"All right!" said Eliza crossly. "Come out!"

Eliza had been right to be suspicious, as out of the corner came... a tall, thin, gangly, slightly hunched little fellow. His legs and arms were impossibly long for such a small chap. Why his hands almost reached past his knees. He was dressed much the same as Gus, the only difference being the shape of his hat

Sebastian

41

and his bright red beard. Eliza stared. Gus in the meantime had unruffled his coat and had shuffled over to the edge of the table.

"Sebastian!" he shouted, jumping up and down. "My dear boy!! Come up! Come up!"

Before Eliza could reach down to help the little man up to the table, he had bounded and bounced his way up, springing from ball, to box, to windowsill, finally jumping down to the tabletop. He moved so quickly she had a difficult time following him. Nonetheless, there he stood, on the corner of the table.

Gus bustled over to the newcomer, clapping him on the back and shaking his hand feverishly.

"Sebastian, Sebastian, my dear boy! How are you? Let me get a look at you? You certainly are a sight for sore eyes! Where are the others? Are they with you?"

Gus was talking so quickly, and firing questions at, who apparently was Sebastian, so rapidly there was not a chance for 'Sebastian' to get a word in. He shook Gus's hand but appeared to be more focused on Eliza. Finally, Gus remembered his manners.

"Eliza, this is my nephew, Sebastian. Sebastian, this is my new friend Eliza. This is her garden and we are in her shed. She is going to help us!" Gus proclaimed proudly.

Eliza reached out with her pinky finger. Sebastian curled his fingers into a fist and nudged the end of her finger. Eliza giggled. Sebastian had fist-pumped her!

"It's very nice to meet you Sebastian," she said.

"Howdy do" said Sebastian.

"Enough, enough!" Gus was getting worked up again. "Where are the others?"

Sebastian turned away from Eliza and put a long, long arm around Gus's shoulders.

"Don't fret old man," said Sebastian. His voice was deep, and he spoke very slowly. It was like watching molasses on a cold morning. His words seemed to hang in the air for ever so long.

"I've come from them. Jenny is finishing the milking. I wish Fritz was here to sort out the earthworms, they seem to always forget how to drive in the rain." The last statement was directed more to Eliza than Gus. "Toad is out looking for you but will meet me back here later, and Snip, I think, is under the pail by the tree. Oh, and by the way, I finished the zip line."

Gus was so relieved all of his family were safe, he gave a huge sigh. "Thank you, Sebastian. I have been so worried. I thought you might all be trapped."

"Why should we be trapped any more than you old Gus? You weren't the only one out working all day." Gus nodded his head in agreement. Of course, it was true. Why hadn't he thought of that!

Satisfied everyone was safe and sound, Gus remembered the problem at hand.

"Right!" exclaimed Gus. "Let's get to work."

Chapter Five

The three friends sat down at the table, Eliza on the milk stool and Sebastian and Gus cross legged on the table. All three stared sadly at the paper. Finally, Eliza picked up a piece of crayon and started to draw. She drew the step which had started the whole adventure. Then she drew the path, the elm tree, the gardens all the way to the back gate and of course, her shed.

Gus and Sebastian watched intently.

Eliza tried to think of all the places in the garden where there might be a good spot to place a door. She drew the stoop her Mother used to hang clothes on the line. Then came the old ladder which leaned against the tool shed, the big, stone fireplace and the box where father kept the firewood. Next came the stack of bricks by the back gate and the pile of old tires next to the drive. Eliza did not think it would be a particularly good place for the door. There was a nasty old rat in the tire pile, so she crossed it off.

Much discussion followed about the pros and cons of each place on the map. Gus was getting quite agitated.

"Excuse me, dear, perhaps I might be able to help?"

The soft, sweet, voice came from the direction of the

windowsill and Eliza looked up from her paper. There stood a lovely, little lady gnome under a tiny flower umbrella. She was dressed similar to the others, but Eliza could see the ruffles from her petticoat peeking out from under the hem of her round, puffy skirt. Her coat was short in the front, almost like a vest, but long in the back as the others, except the coattails curled up ever so slightly. Her hat was bent, presumably so it would fit under the umbrella and came down over her eyes, resting on her nose. On either side of her head were long, long braids of snow-white hair which fell nearly to the ground. Eliza was able to see a bit of her face, or at least her lips under her plump round nose as there were no whiskers to obscure it. Her lips were as red as cherries and she had the pinkest, rosy cheeks you ever did see.

"You must be Jenny" stated Eliza. "won't you come in?"

"Yes dear," said Jenny in a sweet voice that reminded Eliza of honey. "I think I might."

Eliza lifted her hand up to the windowsill as Jenny shook the moisture from her umbrella and closed it. Jenny didn't pause at all but jumped right into the palm of Eliza's upturned hand, her skirts flouncing and poof-ing out around her. Jenny landed in Eliza's palm as lightly as a feather and Eliza slowly lowered her to the table.

No sooner did Jenny's tiny feet hit the top of the table than Gus rushed in and swooped her up in a huge hug, swinging her about in a circle.

"Oh, my Jenny! My Jenny, Jenny". Gus was almost giggling with glee.

Jenny hugged him back and then, remembering they were not alone, quickly admonished Gus to put her

Jenny

down. Gus did as she asked and Jenny, seeing Gus was a bit sad, lifted the brim of his hat and kissed him daintily on the nose. Gus blushed. Sebastian turned away, whistling softly, and shuffling his foot behind the other.

Gus rummaged in the biscuit tin and produced the thread spool for Jenny to sit on. The four of them were about to start work again when they were interrupted.

"G..g..g…g..good mornin'. G..g….g..Gus". This apparently, was Toad, and right behind him, his hand covering a huge yawn, was, Eliza assumed, Snip.

Toad was short and round, dressed the same as the others but his coat appeared a bit snug. Eliza could see the buttons tugging at the delicate fabric as if at any moment, they might pop free of the buttonhole. Snip was taller and a bit slender but not skinny like Sebastian. His coat did not reach the floor. In fact, neither did his pants and Eliza could barely make out his striped socks before they disappeared into the most enormous shoes, well at least for a gnome.

Jenny quickly made introductions and they all gathered around the paper map Eliza had drawn. All of them, except Snip. He was already fast asleep on the table, his head propped against the biscuit tin.

"Don't worry about him, my dear," said Jenny softly. "He works

47

the night shift."

"Really?" said Eliza, a bit startled.

"Yes dear. He is a conductor on the Centipede Rail. They only work nights. He really should be home in bed, but, um….well, you understand dear."

Eliza nodded and reached over and picked up an empty matchbox. She carefully measured the box against a sleeping Snip, then set to work. After peeking in and out of a few of her trinket boxes, she found a wad of lint from the dryer which would make a lovely mattress and carefully folded her handkerchief from her pocket for a warm blanket. She also found a small pompom which would make a dandy pillow for his head. Eliza put it all together and presented the lovely little bed to Jenny. Jenny clapped her hands and Eliza took a quick bow. Toad, Sebastian, and Gus all helped lift a soundly, sleeping Snip into the matchbox bed and Jenny tucked him in. Then they all went back to work on the map.

It wasn't long before Snip was snoring so loudly, the others could barely hear themselves think. Gus was beginning to bluster, and Sebastian had pulled his hat down almost to his shoulders. Jenny and Toad both had their fingers stuck into their ears.

"G..g..g..Gus!" stammered Toad, "d…d…d..do something!"

"I have the perfect thing!" exclaimed Eliza, and lifting the matchbox bed, with the snoring Snip inside, carried him over to the ledge, on the other side of the shed. She opened up an old birthday card of her Mother's and set it up around the box, like a screen. Then she returned to the table.

"Perhaps, we should leave him a note," said Eliza.

"Not to worry, dear," said Jenny. "Snip can't read, and he won't be up for positively hours."

The conversation about the best location for the new door resumed. Problem was, everyone had a completely different opinion of what the best location for the new door would be. The debate had gotten so intense both Gus and Sebastian had resorted to shouting. This would never do. Eliza was about to give up when there came a light tap at the double swing door.

"YooHoo! Eliza, are you in there?" It was Mr. McGuigan. The little gnomes panicked and began running around on top of the table looking for someplace to hide. Eliza shushed them to be quiet and replied.

"Yes, Mr. McGuigan. I'm here."

"Well Lass, your Mother told Mrs. M you needed to see me, and as I am too old and too big to fit into your shed, perhaps you might be so kind as to let me get out of the rain and come over to the workshop? I have a lovely, warm fire burning."

Eliza loved Mr. McGuigan, and Mrs. McGuigan too. She loved how they always seemed to have time for her. Mrs. McGuigan always had her over whenever she baked, to help, and Mr. McGuigan, seemed to never get through a day without needing to tell her at least one story. Father had said Mr. McGuigan's stories were full of blarney. She had no idea what blarney was, but she liked his stories very much. She would often perch on her high stool in his workshop as he fashioned all manners of beautiful things from wood. It was where she had first heard of fairies and gnomes. Mr. McGuigan had told her endless stories about the "wee folk" as he called them. The McGuigan's were from Ireland and although they had lived here many years, still spoke with the soft lilt of Ireland in their voices.

"Yes, Mr. McGuigan. I will be right there, thank you."

The four little gnomes had all lined up, one beside the other on the side of the biscuit tin furthest away from the door. Sebastian, being so tall, was sitting on the table hunched up in a ball, trying his best to stay hidden.

Gus slumped back against the tin.

"Figgerton Fog." He muttered. "I'm too old for this."

"Nonsense," said Eliza. "Mr. McGuigan is the only one who can help! We have to trust him. Besides!" she puffed, "He's Irish!!!"

Eliza emptied the orange crate of books which was sitting on the floor and held it up to her friends.

"All right everybody. Get in. Let's get this show on the road!"

The four little people gathered together in a huddle. Eliza could hear a great deal of muttering and the odd stammer as Toad made his feelings known. Once in awhile, Sebastian would stand up and look at Eliza then go back into the huddle. Finally, they reached a decision.

Gus, as the spokesperson, and as the one who knew Eliza best, approached the edge of the table.

"You made me a promise yesterday Eliza, you wouldn't allow me to be eaten. I am going to hold you to it. Not only for me, but for all of us." Gus was very stern.

"Yes, Gus. Of course. Nothing will happen to any of you and no one is going to be eaten!" Eliza was exasperated.

"And another thing, before you go making excuses, we all know beyond any shadow of a doubt. The McGuigan's have, in their garden, A CAT!!!!" exclaimed Gus with considerable agitation.

The three other little folk huddled together.

"Mr. Jones. He's a frightfully nice, old cat." Explained Eliza, calmly.

"On the contrary, Miss Eliza," said Sebastian. "He may be old, but he is definitely…. frightful! Why he chased me all the way from the hollyhocks to the pea patch on the zip line last week!!!"

"He's r….r…r..right, Miss Eliza. That c…c…c..cat chased me down a row of c…c…c..carrots yesterday!" said Toad, who also appeared to be flustered by the presence of her furry friend.

All the little folk were talking one over the other, telling her of some incident or other they had had, with poor old Mr. Jones. Silly old cat! She would have to give him a talking to.

Mr. Jones was an incredibly old, very large and very broad cat. Eliza doubted old Mr. Jones would be able to move fast enough to chase anything anywhere. He had long white whiskers and Eliza could never tell if he was white with black splotches or black with white splotches. One ear was black, and the other was white and 3 paws had white mittens and one did not. Even his tail was splotchy. He had a mostly white face except for a large black splotch covered one eye and made it look like he was wearing an eye patch. His nose, however, was pink. Still, he was, however, a cat, and as cats are known all the world over for catching mice, occasionally birds, etc., which troubled Eliza quite a bit, there could be some merit to her friend's stories. She would have to be on the lookout for Mr. Jones.

Eliza did her best to reassure her friends and then lifting them one by one, she carefully put them inside the orange crate as it was the only thing she had large enough to hold them all, for her to carry. She then stretched an old shower cap Mrs. McGuigan had thrown out Eliza had rescued from the rubbish, over the top of the crate to keep the rain away. Satisfied her friends were safe and dry. Eliza put on her rain cap and tucking the crate under one arm, set off for Mr. McGuigan's workshop.

Chapter Six

Eliza scurried up the path from her shed to the step of Mr. McGuigan's workshop. She knocked, and then waited with her hand on the worn old metal knob, for permission to go in. The door to the workshop was the oddest door Eliza had ever seen. It was split completely in half, right across the middle. Eliza thought it was a bit silly, but she did like how, when she turned the knob, only the bottom half of the door opened. She could then duck slightly and walk right into the shop without ever having to open the entire door.

"Come in, come in" called Mr. McGuigan, "weather outside is only fit for ducks!"

Eliza could hear Mr. McGuigan chuckling at his joke. She giggled too. She set down the crate, glancing around for the cat and took off her rain cap and coat. She sat down to pull off her galoshes and quickly slipped her feet into the little shoes she kept here, for such an occasion. Picking up the crate, Eliza walked over to give Mr. McGuigan his customary hug. She loved the way she felt swallowed up in Mr. McGuigan's big bear hug. Mr. and Mrs. McGuigan did not have any children and therefore no grandchildren of their own, so they had, as often happens in such cases, adopted the Fitches. They spent all the holidays together and as Eliza had no other Grandparents, she had adopted them right back.

"And what have you there?" said Mr. McGuigan, pointing to the crate she was holding as he picked her up and set her on the tall stool.

"Before I tell you, Mr. McGuigan. Would you be so kind as to say if Mr. Jones is about?" Eliza said, as she looked about the room, trying to spy Mr. Jones in any of his familiar hiding places.

Mr. McGuigan waved his hand. "No, No. This is no weather for that silly old cat. He is likely curled up on Mrs. M's knitting chair sound asleep."

"Well, that's fine then," sighed Eliza with relief.

Then, turning to Mr. McGuigan, Eliza simply stated. "I think, Mr. McGuigan, it would be, a very good idea if you should sit down."

Mr. McGuigan set down his whisk broom he had been cleaning off the workbench with and lifted one hand to remove his glasses and wipe the dust from them with his shirt tail. Mr. McGuigan had extraordinarily bushy eyebrows which peeked out above the wire frames of his glasses. His huge smile and jolly cheeks and the ever-present twinkle in his eyes always made him look like he knew the answer to a good many jokes and riddles. He was one of Eliza's favorite people and she loved him dearly.

Mr. McGuigan teased Eliza dreadfully, and was about to again but he looked at Eliza for a moment and seeing she was quite determined, sat down on his own tall stool.

"Thank you," said Eliza politely. Then she sat her little crate on the workbench and slowly lifted off the shower cap.

"Mr. McGuigan, I would very much like for you to meet my new friends. They need your help."

Slowly, and carefully, Eliza reached into the crate and lifted each of her friends gently onto the workbench, introducing them politely as she did. Mr. McGuigan sat back quite astonished and rubbed his eyes under the wire rim of his glasses, over and over as if he were having a hard time believing what he was seeing. He sat for a moment, trying to take it all in and then jumped up dancing around the shop.

"Leprechauns!!" he squealed. "I knew they were real".

Mr. McGuigan did his best rendition of a jig and then, all out of breath came back and plopped back onto his stool. Taking a handkerchief out of his pocket, he wiped his face and his eyes which Eliza thought were surprisingly moist. Her friends looked from one to the other and shrugged their shoulders not knowing what else to do or what to make of Mr. McGuigan's reaction.

"No Mr. McGuigan," said Eliza softly. "These are gnomes. They live under my garden stairs."

Mr. McGuigan stopped for a moment and considered what Eliza had said. Suddenly, he leaned forward and whispered.

"The back-garden stairs?" he asked. Eliza nodded. "The new or the old?" asked Mr. McGuigan.

"The old" Eliza said.

"OH," said Mr. McGuigan.

Gus finally worked up his nerve and bustled forward, standing in front of Mr. McGuigan.

"Excuse me, Sir," he said in his low gruff voice but trying hard to be polite. "Do you think you can help us? You see, what we very much need, is a new door."

Mr. McGuigan sat for a moment, then jumped up and began frantically looking through the shelves on the side of the workbench.

"It's here somewhere" he muttered. "Where in tarnation have I put it."

Eliza had no idea what Mr. McGuigan was looking for, but

he was definitely looking for something very particular. Gus and the others watched as Mr. McGuigan pulled first one book then another, out of the shelves and then rammed them back in and continued his search.

By the time Mr. McGuigan stopped for a breath, the workshop was filled with dust. Jenny coughed softly.

"Mr. McGuigan," asked Eliza, "what are you looking for? Perhaps, if we were to help, we might be able to find it."

Mr. McGuigan stopped and taking the handkerchief out of his pocket, rubbed his face and the back of his neck, and then, much to Eliza's delight, opened the handkerchief and placed it on the top of his head, the corners dipping down on either side of his glasses. He looked very silly.

"It can't hurt," he said with a chuckle. "Mrs. M is always after me to clean out my workshop, but then I mention her sewing room, and it seems to do the trick!" Mr. McGuigan grinned. "I am looking for a large, old book. It is bright green, or at least it used to be, probably faded by now. It has gold writing and I would imagine", he paused as if deep in thought, "it will be covered by quite a lot of dust!"

The friends set to work. Each of them taking a different shelf along the wall of the workshop. At one point, Toad took rather a nasty tumble, as he was so roly-poly and round, it was difficult for him to walk along the lip of the shelf. Eliza was shocked to see when he hit the top of the workbench, he bounced! Still, Eliza dashed over to make sure he was quite alright and seeing he was no worse for wear, went back to work. Toad decided to search the low shelves, closer to the floor.

They had been searching for quite a long time when, from under the workbench, there was a bit of scuffling, and Toad emerged, covered in dust-bunnies and cobwebs.

"S...s...s...stop" he shouted! "I think I have f...f...f..found it!"

Eliza was on top of the workbench and she laid down and looked over the edge. Toad was doing his best to dust himself off, clapping his hands against his coat, little tufts of dust filling the air around him. Sebastian, who was on the very top shelf, bounded and bounced his way down to assist. Jenny sneezed.

Gus bustled over to where Eliza lay, her pigtails falling in front of her face.

"What's this?" he blustered, "what do you say? What did you find?"

Mr. McGuigan got down from the ladder he was standing on and came over. Eliza sat up and lifted Gus up and Mr. McGuigan carefully lifted the two of them down to the floor. Mr. McGuigan was much too old and stiff to be down on all fours under the workbench, so Eliza, being much closer to the ground anyway, knelt down to peer into the dark, dusty spot Toad had pointed to.

"Well," she said, "it certainly is very dusty, and there does appear to be something quite large back there, but I am not sure I will be able to reach it!"

Eliza got up and dusted herself off. It was a workshop after all, so it wasn't bound to be as clean as a house and there were all sorts of bits of wood shavings and sawdust under the workbench Mr. McGuigan had missed when he had swept up. Eliza giggled to herself. Some of the wood shavings had been there for quite a long time.

Suddenly, there was a great deal of huffing and puffing and Eliza looked down to see her friends pushing and pulling and tugging at the big heavy book. It was taking a great deal of effort for such little folk. Finally, Jenny, waving her arms, brought everyone to a halt.

"Mr. McGuigan" she huffed, short of breath, "might you have a decent-sized feather about? There is such a lot of dust and wood-shavings down here, perhaps it would go better if I could get it swept up a bit."

Mr. McGuigan looked around the workshop and then trumped over to the far corner. He rustled around in a small pail and with a very pronounced "just the thing" turned and with a great flourish, presented Jenny with a lovely long, stiff, pigeon feather.

"Here ye be wee Jenny," he said.

"Thanks very much, dear," said Jenny. "That should do nicely."

Jenny scurried under the workbench and set about clearing a path for the big book. Dust and wood curls and sawdust puffed out from under the workbench and then with a great deal more huffing and puffing, slowly appeared the corner of a large, incredibly old, very faded, bright green book with gold letters.

Eliza stooped over and struggling with the weight, managed to pick it up enough Mr. McGuigan could get a hold of it. He picked it up and dropped it on the workbench with a thump. Eliza picked up each of her little friends and set them on the workbench beside the book, then Mr. McGuigan picked up Eliza and set her gently on her stool. All were present and accounted for, except of course for Snip, who was still fast asleep in the matchbox in the shed.

Mr. McGuigan was about to open the big book, but Jenny stopped him.

"Just a moment dear," she said softly, patting Mr. McGuigan's arm "might you give me a hand?"

Mr. McGuigan opened his big hand and with Gus giving her a courteous hand up, Jenny signaled she was ready. Mr. McGuigan lifted Jenny, with her feather, up onto the front cover of the book where she set about quickly and thoroughly dusting it off. Once she was satisfied it was genuinely clean, she nodded her approval and then was gently set back down on the workbench.

Ever so slowly, Mr. McGuigan lifted the front cover. The gold writing on the cover was nothing Eliza had ever seen before. It looked like words but, as she could not yet read, it was awfully hard to tell. It did not, however, look like any of the letters in any of her storybooks.

"Mr. McGuigan?" asked Eliza softly.

"Yes lass" he replied.

"What does it say?"

Mr. McGuigan took out his handkerchief and polished the front of the book a bit more. His eyes were not as good as they used to be, and the light was a bit dim.

"It says Aos Si... it means this is a book about the wee folk. It is in Gaelic, the traditional language of Ireland and Scotland. Well then," he said in a hushed voice, "would ye all be ready to see what's inside?"

Mr. McGuigan gathered everyone closely around and moved the heavy book up so it was leaning against the shelf and everyone could see. Slowly, he opened the front cover and began to turn the pages. Eliza's eyes grew big as she looked upon pages and pages of drawings of "little people". They looked similar to her new friends in height, but there were definitely some noticeable, differences. Most of the people on the pages had very pointy ears and were d r e s s e d in vastly different clothes.

F i r s t came elves,

like the ones you see at Christmas, dressed all in red and green, with curly toed shoes and pointy hats which were much shorter than any of the hats her gnomes were wearing.

Then came pages and pages of leprechauns all dressed in little suits with short pants and white stockings and wonderful black shoes with shiny buckles. All the leprechauns had fancy top hats, with red curly hair poking out beneath and freckles, much like Eliza's, sprinkled across their noses. Mr. McGuigan had certainly read these pages many times, as there was a beautiful, faded, old bookmark tucked into the first page. The pages were slightly worn, and the corners a bit damaged. Yes. Mr. McGuigan had read these pages many, many times.

Next came the trolls. Eliza was not as fond of the trolls as she felt they looked to gruff to be friendly. Gus agreed with her, certain kinds of trolls could be most difficult indeed. However, Jenny was quick to correct him. She felt, trolls, for the most part, were simply misunderstood.

Pages and pages went by until finally, Sebastian with a shout exclaimed, "There we are! That's us!"

Sure enough, on the pages before them were drawings which could have easily been any one of the four little people standing on the workbench. The title at the top of the page was "Scandinavian Garden, Forest, and Woodland Gnomes".

Eliza had no idea there were so very many different types of gnomes. She looked at all the pictures. It almost appeared to be like a family album of her gnomes. There were more as well. All had the same plump nose, the same long pointy hats, and remarkably similar whiskers. Toad giggled as they turned the pages. "That looks like S.. s...s...Simpkin!" the rest roared with laughter. "Look, there's F...f....f...Filbert, Naoimi and F..f...f...Fart!"

"Not Fart, dear," said Jenny, holding her sides as she laughed "It's Bart, dear".

Sebastian was rolling on the workbench laughing and Gus had tears rolling down his whiskers and was leaning against Mr. McGuigan's arm for support. Even Mr. McGuigan was chuckling and Eliza herself had caught a bad case of the giggles.

Jenny proceeded to explain why some of the gnomes had different clothes. "These" she simply stated "with the lovely plaid fabric, are country gnomes. They look after farm gardens, and the wildflowers growing along the lanes."

Eliza nodded she understood.

"These," said Jenny, pointing to the gnomes that seemed to be dressed in the prickly evergreen branches like the tree Father got at Christmas, "these are forest gnomes, they look after all the small creatures in the forest. They must blend into the trees so they can't be spotted by owls."

"I say" said Mr. McGuigan "how very clever."

Mr. McGuigan turned another page. Jenny explained each and every one, and how you can tell the difference by what they wear. There were gnomes who tended all the wee flowers in the far north. They were dressed mostly in bits and pieces of fur they had picked up when foxes and rabbits changed their coats in the fall and the spring.

Eliza's favorites were the Dutch gnomes with their little wooden shoes. They specialized in opening tulips, which was, according to Gus, extremely difficult because the tulips flowers were so far off the ground. They could be found anywhere in the world early in the spring when tulips first began to grow. They would stay until the tulips season was over, then return back to the Neverlands. Gus explained although the country of Holland was often referred to as the Netherlands, where the gnomes lived, was called the Neverlands.

There were gnomes dressed in clothes from around the world, but all their hats and whiskers were similar, regardless of the style of clothes they wore.

Eliza was fascinated by all the pictures of gnome beds, and furniture and all sorts of swings and things. Finally, Mr. McGuigan turned the next page and there in front of them, were doors. There were doors into the sides of sheds, doors fixed to fences and doors for the side of big rocks. The following page had doors for going under flower boxes, doors that went straight underground and doors into the side of plant pots.

Then on the next to last page, came the most beautiful doors Eliza had ever seen. These were the doors her four little friends were the most interested in. These were doors that could go on a tree.

"I don't understand," Eliza said simply "you mean you can only put a certain kind of door in a certain place? Won't any door do?"

Gus began to bluster.

"No, No, No," he fumed, "it doesn't work like that! We cannot put any old door anywhere! Don't be ridiculous!" he huffed.

Jenny shushed him gently. "Don't mind him" she smiled, patting Gus on the hand. "No dear. We cannot use just any door. The magic only works if we put the right door in the right place."

"Magic?" said Eliza and Mr. McGuigan, both at the same time and both quite incredulously.

"Magic" stated Jenny with a nod. "How else do you think a plain door will open?"

Mr. McGuigan and Eliza looked at each other with wonder. They had not even thought there could be magic. Eliza clapped her hands with delight.

"Oh please, Jenny. Do tell us more."

All the little folk rushed forwards, talking all in a jumble and quite impossible to make out. Finally, Gus took charge.

"Ahem!" he shouted. "If you don't mind, I will explain." The rest of the little folk submitted and took a step back giving Gus an air of importance and centre stage.

"It's like this. Every door is built for, and only suits, one particular place. The type of material used and how it is put together determines where it should be. As you can see from these pictures, which are remarkably accurate," he said more in wonder to the others, who all nodded in agreement, "the most beautiful doors, are the only ones fit for trees. None of the others would ever open if propped against a tree." The others nodded again.

"Well" stated Eliza matter of fact-ly. "Then we shall have to build you one of the most beautiful doors ever, and you can put it against any tree you choose."

The gnomes seemed to simply buzz with excitement, and they all began chattering and talking at once.

"B…b….b….but it's not that simple" stammered Toad.

"Why ever not?" asked Eliza.

"Because it's not simple!" shouted Gus. Eliza looked like she might cry, she was only trying to help.

"Now, now, dear," Jenny said "don't fret. You see, in order for a door to be made for a tree, all the wood in the door must come from that tree, and it is sometimes very difficult to do, because you can only use the wood and bark and twigs and things the tree gives you willingly, and most trees, are rather stingy and tend not to give up bits of themselves, not that I can blame them."

The others nodded again.

Eliza was about to ask another question when there was a knock at the door and before Mr. McGuigan could so much as answer the door flew open and in puffed Mrs. McGuigan, along with old Mr. Jones. Mrs. McGuigan had a large basket over her arm and Mr. Jones shuffled in, shaking the moisture from his coat as Mrs. McGuigan shook the rain off her umbrella and laid it aside, next to the little potbellied stove to dry.

The little gnomes were frozen in spot for a few seconds then all began to dash about, searching for somewhere to hide. Mr. McGuigan thought fast and placed a box over the book and tucked each of their new friends inside.

"Well you two, Mr. M., did you not take heed of the time? This poor child must be fainting from hunger!"

Mr. McGuigan looked a bit perplexed, then with a shaky hand, reaching into his pocket and pulled out his pocket watch. "Good heavens, Mother. Why didn't you say something!"

"Oh posh!" said Mrs. McGuigan, then shook her head and began emptying out the contents of her basket.

"I have already told your Mother you are welcome here for lunch Eliza. It's far to wet out for you to be running back and forth for the want of a cucumber sandwich and I told her the two of you were obviously hard at work and busy with whatever it is you are up to and I would simply bring you out something as Mr. M. would be likely needing something as well."

Mrs. McGuigan did have a habit of running on a bit when she talked, and Eliza loved how she would keep going and going. She seemed to need hardly ever even to draw a breath. She had heard Mrs. M. and her Mother chatting over the fence many times and it had always been a source of wondering for her, how they managed to hear what the other was saying when they were both talking, and neither was listening.

Meanwhile, Mr. Jones, having shaken all the moisture from his thick coat, and licking his paws dry, had proceeded to rub against Eliza's leg letting her know he was in the mood to be cuddled. Eliza was one of his favorite people and as she did love to give him a great deal of cuddles and snuggles, could not understand why on earth she hadn't done so.

Eliza looked at Mr. McGuigan and then knowingly at the box and then back again. Mr. McGuigan, winked, then lifting a rather large toolbox he set it down right on top of the box. Mrs. McGuigan was still busily laying out their lunch, so did not seem to notice a thing. Eliza scooped up Mr. Jones and hugging him close, settled on her stool. Mrs. McGuigan was setting out such a scrumptious lunch and as Eliza looked on, she began laying out lovely cucumber sandwiches, crusts cut off as is only proper. There were deviled eggs, one of Eliza's favorites, as well as carrot sticks and celery, radishes for Mr. McGuigan and two large glasses and a sealer jar of milk. To top it all off, some fresh-baked oatmeal cookies, which happened to be Eliza's favorites.

"You didn't bring a glass for you" commented Eliza.

"Oh," said Mrs. McGuigan. "I am not about to interfere with whatever the two of you are up to out here on this soggy day. No, Mr. Jones and I will go back up to the house and leave the two of you to your shenanigans."

Mr. Jones had enjoyed the cuddles and the scratches under the chin from Eliza but had also begun to take a fair bit of interest in the box. He had begun sniffing and squirming and was becoming quite difficult for Eliza to hold.

Mrs. McGuigan scolded the old cat and placed him right on top of the workbench. Eliza held her breath and with a pleading look, stared at Mr. McGuigan. Mr. Jones began sniffing at the box.

"Git away, ole cat," said Mr. McGuigan, giving the old cat a bit of a push.

"Now, now" scolded Mrs. McGuigan. "he isn't hurting a thing. Come on, Mr. Jones, we are obviously not wanted here!"

"Thank you for lunch Mrs. McGuigan," said Eliza politely. Mrs. McGuigan kissed her on the cheek, plucked Mr. Jones off the workbench and set him on the floor, patting him on the bottom lightly so he would head toward the door. She picked up her umbrella and tossing Eliza a kiss, was out the door and on her way up to the house, ushering Mr. Jones in front of her.

As soon as she was out of the workshop, Mr. McGuigan lifted the toolbox off the box and lifted the box off their friends.

"I don't mind tellin' you Mr. McGuigan," said Sebastian, "that cat was close enough to make it uncomfortable."

Mr. McGuigan waved his hand, "I'd not be letting any harm be comin' to you" he chuckled. "Now! Let's eat!"

Chapter Seven

Sebastian was already wandering through the plates and bowls of food laid out on the table, sniffing intently. Eliza picked up a couple of napkins and opened them up as a picnic tablecloth. Mr. McGuigan took out his pocketknife and carefully cut up some of the sandwiches and vegetables into more, gnome friendly, portions. Using a slice of cucumber as a plate, Jenny daintily handed each of the small gentlemen their lunch. Mr. McGuigan even managed to find some small bottle caps which worked remarkably well for cups. Eliza broke up one of the cookies to share.

The friends munched and chatted. There was ever so much to learn, and Eliza had so many questions about all the pictures she had seen. The conversation continued, and even though Mr. McGuigan occasionally sat back on his stool scratching his partially bald head with some new information to process, seemed every bit to have had a dream come true.

Gus had taken quite a liking to her old friend and took the time to discuss the more technical intricacies of the tools and furnishings they used. Mr. McGuigan was all ears as their friends continued to delight them both with stories from their world.

Lunch finished, Eliza quickly tidied up and the friends went back to work. Finally, after much more discussion about the doors, Mr. McGuigan sat back on his stool, wiping his face, head, and neck with his handkerchief.

"Well then," said Mr. McGuigan with a sigh. "It sounds to me like you wee folk, are decided then. We must find a lovely big tree who will give us all the bits to build a door with. Any ideas?"

"What about the big tree in my garden?" asked Eliza with a shout. "That would be the perfect tree as we can visit ever so often and I would know you are there and you could come into the shed and we could have tea, and on really cold days, you could all come into the house to my room and stay in the little dollhouse!" Eliza was so excited she was bouncing and dancing around the room as she talked.

Jenny and Gus looked at each other with concern. The others nodded in agreement.

"Well you see Dear," said Jenny. "Mr. Ulmus isn't particularly pleasant to deal with and he has said no many times. That's why our door was in your step."

The other's stood, sadly nodding in agreement.

"Mr. Ulmus?" said Eliza.

"Yes Dear. That's his name." said Jenny patiently.

"Whose name?" said Eliza

"The tree in your garden, Dear. Ulmus is the scientific name for elm tree."

Eliza and Mr. McGuigan looked at each other and blinked.

"But what do you mean he isn't pleasant? You mean he won't allow you to put a door on him?" Eliza was quite provoked about this bit of news. Stuffy old tree! Who did he think he was?

The gnomes nodded sadly.

"Well!" said Mr. McGuigan. "We'll have to see about that!"

A debate began about what would be the best way to go about asking a grumpy old tree, to allow some very nice gnomes to put a door against it. Then of course, how to ask the same grumpy old tree, to give up bits of himself, to make the door in the first place.

Mr. McGuigan had started to make some inquiries as to how much wood they would need and the dimensions of the door they would require.

"Well" stated Gus, "do remember not all the bits need to be from the old tree, only the main parts. We can decorate it and use a few bits and pieces from other places as we see fit. There must be nothing man-made, however, or it will not work. Everything must be from the natural world".

It made perfect sense to Mr. McGuigan, but he assured them, as he had been a very good carpenter, he felt he would be able to make the door without the need for nails or anything of the like.

It was decided, perhaps, seeing as it was her garden, Eliza, accompanied by Jenny, should make the first request regarding being allowed to actually set a door against the old tree. The further request, about being allowed to perhaps use bits of the old tree, would be left until the first request was agreed to. The friends thought, since it had been many years since any such request had been made, perhaps the old elm tree had forgotten. It was also thought perhaps, he had also improved in temper, however, it was considered to be highly unlikely, by the gnomes.

It was also decided that once permission was in fact secured, Mr. McGuigan should make the door.

There was much discussion, followed by much more discussion, as well as more than a few objections, from Gus. It was not until Eliza's father had called from outside the workshop that any of them realized how late it had become.

"Eliza" her father called. "It really is time you came home. Mr. McGuigan must be allowed to go into the house for dinner."

This startled everyone in the workshop and sent a flurry of jostling and running about. "Yes, Father," Eliza called, hoping to stop him from opening the door. "I'll be home directly!"

This response seemed to be what Father was looking for and footsteps could be heard going away from the workshop.

Mr. McGuigan took out his handkerchief again, to wipe his brow. The whole day had been quite exhausting, and Mr. McGuigan certainly felt in need of a nap. It was his regular habit as it was, but today, it was really needed!

Eliza loaded all her little friends into her crate, carefully covering them with the shower cap, slipped back into her raincoat, hat and galoshes prepared to head out of the workshop and back to her shed. She needed to carefully, collect a snoring Snip, who was still fast asleep.

With a final big bear hug from Mr. McGuigan and many, many thanks to him from Gus, Jenny, Toad and Sebastian, Eliza gathered up her little friends and made her way back to her shed. It really was beginning to storm quite frightfully now, and the wind pushed her back and forth along the path until she got to the two-way door of her shed. There were even a few times she was dreadfully afraid the wind might tear the little crate out of her hands, to say nothing of pulling her lovely rain hat off her head.

She had to fight the wind quite hard in fact, to open the

little door into her shed. Once done, she quickly went inside and closed it with a good push. She set the little crate on the table and quickly popped off the shower cap to check on her friends.

It had been a fairly tumultuous trip from Mr. McGuigan's workshop to Eliza's shed. The wind had jostled her quite badly as she had made her way down the pathway and she had found it, more than a little difficult, to keep her balance and stay on her feet. The stones making up the pathway could get quite slippery when they were wet, and it had been raining quite a lot all day so there was a fair bit of mud about too.

Gus and Jenny were huddled together at one end of the crate. Sebastian was sitting with his long legs stretched out in front of him, his back on one side of the crate and his large feet, pressed against the other. Toad, unfortunately, had faired the worst and as he was so roly-poly was, well, basically, upside down in the other corner.

Eliza helped him right himself and lifted all her friends out of the crate. Jenny quickly set to work helping everyone straighten their clothes, hats, and whiskers.

"G…g…g..goodness!" exclaimed Toad.

"I'm so sorry Mr. Toad," said Eliza, trying to apologize for the bumpy ride.

"Don't worry my dear," said Jenny. "It's getting so stormy out we may have to re-think our plan."

The others nodded in agreement. It really was getting extremely stormy and as Eliza was about to agree there was a huge clap of thunder. The thunder shook the little shed and made everyone jump.

"Hello!! What's happening! Where the devil am I!"

Came a somewhat sleepy, startled voice from behind the birthday card screen. Eliza carefully lifted Snip, in his matchbox bed, down off the shelf.

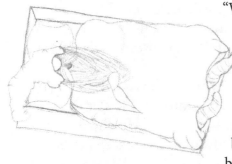

"What's going on! What is happening! Somebody tell me where the devil I am!" Snip was really agitated, and Eliza could certainly understand why having been waken so suddenly by such a loud boom of thunder.

"I am sorry Mr. Snip," said Eliza politely. "It must have been a shock to wake up somewhere so unfamiliar. You see, you had fallen asleep here on the table when you came in earlier, and as... um... as it was, ... um," Eliza was trying to find a polite way to tell Snip how he had come to be on the shelf in a matchbox without being rude about his snoring.

"Oh, GILDERFLIXES!" blustered Gus, "you were snoring so loud we could not think! So, Miss Eliza here, made you this lovely bed and we stuffed you in it, and she put you up on the shelf so we could have some peace and quiet!"

Snip was sitting up in bed, trying with some difficulty to wake up completely, still obviously confused as to what had gone on.

"It's t...t....t...true" said Toad.

Jenny nodded. Then sitting on the edge of the bed, proceeded to give Snip an abbreviated version of the day's events. Snip could only stare at his friends in wonder and still being a bit confused, was about to start to ask questions.

"ELIZA!! ELIZA... YOU MUST COME IN!"

Father's voice could barely be heard over the wind.

Eliza started at the sound and quickly answered.

"I'm coming" she had to shout to be heard, which made her friends all quickly cover their ears.

"Sorry" she whispered. She then carefully, went about lifting each of the little men into the crate and quickly covered it with the shower cap. It was really raining hard now, and she wanted to make sure her friends did not get wet. Jenny then became the sole occupant of the handbag.

It had been decided that Jenny and Eliza were to speak to Mr. Ulmus on their way back up to the house. Jenny and Gus did not have high hopes he might say yes, but they had decided to try regardless. However, it was far too blustery and nasty to do so today, so the friends had agreed they should wait until the storm passed, and perhaps, make an attempt, later in the evening.

Eliza hurried up the path to the house, trying her best not to jostle her friends in the crate too badly as she fought against the wind and rain until she finally reached the shelter of the house. It really was very nasty and what had been such a lovely rain this morning, was turning into a fairly, ferocious storm which looked like it might last all night!

Eliza needed to put the crate between her feet so she could use both hands to open the door against the wind. Her galoshes and her raincoat provided a bit more protection for the crate, but not enough to save the shower cap from being torn off. Sebastian acted quickly and managed to grab a handful of the cap, and with Gus, Snip and Toad hanging onto him were able to keep Sebastian from being blown away. Eliza managed to get the backdoor open, then the inside door and then bustled herself, and the crate and the handbag all inside the door at once. She quickly covered the crate again and shut the door with a bang.

"Lands sakes Eliza!" exclaimed her father, popping his head around the corner.

"I'm sorry Father," said Eliza "the wind!"

"What kept you out all day. You must not take advantage of Mr. McGuigan so. Perhaps he had work to do!"

"I'm sorry Father," Eliza said softly "we were reading a book."

"Oh well then, no wonder the two of you lost track of time. Good story was it?" her father asked.

"It was an excellent story" beamed Eliza "it was all about the little folk."

Her father nodded his head and smiled. Mr. McGuigan's fondness for such stories was legendary and if it was what they were reading, it was easy to see how they might have lost complete track of time. Eliza was, at 6 and ¾ and 3 days old, the perfect audience for Mr. McGuigan and as it had poured all day, her father acknowledged she may as well have been listening to a good story with such a good friend as Mr. McGuigan as fretting about the house she couldn't be out in the garden.

"And what have you there in your little crate?" asked father with a questioning look.

"OH" Eliza had to think fast. "oh, only some treasures from my shed" she stated as matter-of-factly as she could.

"Well then," he teased, "best whisk them up to your room before your mother catches you".

It was a well-known rule, in her house, once treasures went out to the shed, they were not to be brought back in again, although the rule seemed only to apply to Mother. Father was more apt to allow the occasional transgression, as long as Eliza made sure to check there were no bugs about. Mice... were also not allowed.

Eliza nodded, and tucking her crate under her arm and gently picking up the handbag, she scooted past Father who was keeping watch on the kitchen door and slipped quietly and quickly up the stairs to her room. She pushed her door mostly closed with her toe, then leaned against it to close it completely. The little house was still as it had been this morning, and Eliza set the crate on the floor and then set about un-bundling Jenny. Ladies first, after all.

Setting Jenny on the table in front of the little house, she turned her attention to the crate and one by one set the little group on the table as well. Gus, now the expert on the little house, having been a guest there already himself, welcomed the others with great gusto.

"Come in, come in" he gushed.

The others seemed as overwhelmed by the little house as Gus had been. Jenny bustled from room to room admiring each room in turn. Eliza had moved her box from the closet closer for them, and the menfolk set about moving in more of the furniture into the house as Jenny directed them as to where each item should be placed. Before long, the little house looked quite comfy.

"Eliza" her mother called, "time for dinner." Mother's voice always had a sing-song sound to it and today was no different.

"I'm coming, Mother" Eliza replied, trying her best to be equally sing-song-ie.

Then she whispered to her friends, "you make yourselves quite at home and I shall fetch something for your dinner, although I am not sure what we are having."

"Not to worry, yourself Dear," said Jenny gently. "Anything will do. We aren't the least bit fussy."

"B...b...b...but Jenny" stammered Toad, "I'm h...h... h... hungry!"

Jenny shushed him sternly.

"You are always hungry Toad!" exclaimed Sebastian, "that's why you are so round!"

The other friends giggled, and Toad looked a bit offended, then started chuckling too.

"R...r..r...right you are, old man!"

Eliza reached over and flicked on the little battery candle that formed a fireplace in the little parlour. Then seeing her friends, settled cozily in front, with Gus already beginning to nod off, scooted down to dinner.

Chapter Eight

Father held Eliza's chair steady as she climbed up to the table. Mother had been busy, and as she often did on rainy days, had prepared what appeared to Eliza to be a feast! OH! Toad would be beside himself to see all the yummy-ness on the table! She carefully folded her paper napkin, very politely, across her lap, as she had been taught to do, then, when Father went into the kitchen to help her mother, folded two more the same way. That way she thought, she might be better able to slip some food into the napkins without being discovered, and it would be easy to tuck it under her shirt to take up to her friends.

Father began to carry in plates and bowls, steaming with delicious things to eat. Eliza sniffed appreciatively. There were lovely fresh buns, still warm from the oven. Corn on the cob steamed from a plate and there were tiny, new potatoes covered in cream and dill. Eliza licked her lips. Mother bustled in from the kitchen, with a huge plate of crispy, golden chicken.

Her original plan was to tuck things into her napkin by spilling them off her plate. Eliza was not sure it was going to work so well with all these yummy things, so she thought she might need to think of another idea, and quickly! It was then, as she was wondering, that she came up with the perfect plan.

Father began dishing up and putting a spoonful of everything onto Eliza's plate.

"If you wouldn't mind, Father," she said, "I am ever so hungry. May I have an extra portion of everything?"

Father looked at her, with raised eyebrows, then glanced at Mother as well. Eliza did not often finish her plate, so for her to ask for extra, seemed a bit odd.

"Didn't you have lunch Eliza?" asked Mother, somewhat perplexed.

"Oh yes," replied Eliza, "but it was ever such a long time ago, and I usually have a snack in between, but I did not have a snack today, we were so busy in the woodshop that I forgot!"

Father was satisfied with her answer, and dutifully, gave Eliza extra portions of everything on the table. Eliza stared at the mountain of food on her plate, and as she really was very hungry, thought she might be able to eat enough that her parents would not be suspicious. Dinner passed with her telling her parents about all the wonderful things she had seen in Mr. McGuigan's book. As it was a real book, she did not think she would be giving away any secrets.

Her parents finished their meal and began to clean up. Now, was her chance. Every time her parents left the table, Eliza would slip something from her plate, and even off a couple of dishes on the table, into the napkins on her lap. A couple of buns, a cob of corn, two drumsticks, and five little potatoes, with as little sauce as she could manage, were carefully bundled into the napkins. This done, Eliza's plate was indeed, quite empty and Eliza's tummy, as well as her lap, was quite full.

Her parents were indeed surprised to see her empty plate and praising her for doing such a good job at finishing her supper, was allowed two brownies for dessert. One, of course, she dropped into her lap. As an extra reward, her Mother cleared her plate, as she was so pleased that Eliza had eaten, what she thought, was an enormous dinner. As soon as her mother left the room to begin the washing up, Eliza bundled her treasure under her shirt and scampered back up to her room.

Jenny had been busy as well. With the help of the menfolk, they had pulled the dining table and chairs, out of the house and had it all set, sitting in front of the little house, on the table. Jenny had felt it would be rude of them to take what food Eliza brought them, and then go back into the house to eat. She had arranged it so Eliza, even though she had finished her supper, could be part of the conversation with them, as they ate theirs.

Sebastian was all but drooling as Eliza began to unwrap the delicious goodies she had scavenged from the table. Toad was sniffing appreciatively, and Gus roused from his nap, sniffed the air intently as he bustled out to the table.

The doll dishes worked quite well as Eliza did her best to divide the meal into smaller portions that the gnomes could manage. She found it quite surprising how big her food looked on the little plates when it had looked so much smaller on hers. Nevertheless, her little friends filled their plates with gusto and settled in for a fine dinner. Eliza really did not know if this was the kind of food they ate, but it was the only kind of food she had, so it would have to do. Taking a moment, she began to wonder, and then, after a moment or two of wondering, decided she needed to know and so, began to ask questions.

"Jenny, would you be so kind as to tell me…is this the type of food you eat, or do you have different food?"

Jenny put down her little fork and wiped her mouth with the tiny bit of napkin Eliza had torn off the bigger one.

"No Dear, this isn't much like our regular food, but it is really delicious, and we have enjoyed it immensely. We normally eat mushrooms, berries, and vegetables your father grows in the garden. We often have roots and things that we make into what you would call a stew. We do eat nuts and seeds as well. Pumpkin seeds are a great delicacy, as are sunflower seeds we roast."

Eliza was fascinated.

"Yum!" she declared, for she liked pumpkin seeds and sunflower seeds as well.

"In the fall," Jenny continued, "we gather all the nuts, acorns, and such and put them in our storeroom. They keep very well, and we will have food over the long winter. We also gather up all the bits of potato, carrots, and things from the vegetable garden that you humans leave behind. Sometimes, it can be a great lot of food! We understand much of it is too small for you to use, but it is perfectly sized for us, so we make sure nothing goes to waste."

Eliza was delighted by all the new information.

"On exceedingly rare occasions, we receive the odd few eggs, or even perhaps a bit of sausage" the men all nodded enthusiastically, "but those are rare indeed and so we make do with what we have."

Eliza thought it would be a particularly good idea if she were to remember to make sure to provide a bit more food for the gnomes, particularly when they were no longer residing in her little house.

"Sebastian, scoundrel that he is," continued Jenny, "occasionally pinches the sausage and eggs out of your mother's grocery bags when she isn't looking or is taking the first lot to the house." She looked at Sebastian crossly. "He has even occasionally, I must confess, pinched some out of your poor father's lunch bucket!"

Laughter bubbled up inside Eliza. She could picture

Sebastian bounding in and out of the back of Mother's car, so quickly with his arms full.

Sebastian simply shrugged his shoulders and grinned. That is when Toad spoke up.

"Your m...m...m...Mother, d...d...d..does make d..d..d... delicious c...c...cookies!" he exclaimed, "the g...g...g... gingersnaps are my f...f...f..favorite!" he pronounced with a grin, rubbing his round tummy with a pudgy hand.

Eliza had no inkling the gnomes would have any idea about any of this and it was quite a wonderment she had never even noticed them before and here she was, finding out they had been pinching sausages and eggs and cookies and heaven knows what else. It made her happy her little friends had been part of her world for so long, and she had not even known it. She was going to make sure she would leave things out for them so Sebastian would not need to run the risk of being caught.

Dinner over, Jenny and Eliza quickly tidied up to make sure there was nothing left out. It was soon time for Mother to come up to tuck Eliza into bed. They had barely finished, the little folk retired back into the little house when there was a soft rap at the door and Mother came in to help Eliza get ready for bed. First, she would need a bath, then her hair washed and combed, then teeth brushed and at last a lovely clean nightgown. Mother then pulled a large book off the shelf in Eliza's room and sitting in the beautiful old rocking chair, lifted Eliza up onto her lap and tucked a soft blanket around her. She then began to read her a story.

Eliza had giggled softly to herself when she had glanced over to see what the little folk were about, to see a row of round noses, poking out of the windows of the little house, as they listened to the story as well.

The story was one of Eliza's favorites. It was all about the

fairies that lived in a garden far, far away. It was her very own story. Her grandmother had written if for her before she was even born and it, along with a number of her grandmother's other stories, had been made into a book. Eliza knew the words almost by heart, but still, it was awfully nice to be snuggled on Mother's lap, listening to her read.

When the story was finished, Mother gave her a big hug, then carried her to her bed and helped her snuggle under the covers, tucking her hair behind her ear, and gave her a kiss on her head. This was always Eliza's favorite part of the day, and even though she would often slip out of bed to the back step to do some wondering, she still loved being tucked in every night the way she always had.

Father came in right behind and gave her a kiss on the cheek and a quick tickle, then pushed the bed covers in around her so tight, she could barely wiggle. That was part of bedtime too and Eliza loved it equally as much.

Father always said, "goodnight, sleep tight, don't let the bed bugs bite, and if they do, take your shoe..." to which Eliza would practically yell "AND BEAT THEM TIL THEY'RE BLACK AND BLUE!!"

Then Father would turn out the light and softly close the door.

Eliza needed to do a fair bit of wiggling to loosen the bedsheets enough she could prop herself up on her elbows and look over at the little house. She could see they had also turned out the lights and she could hear some snoring coming from the direction of the bedroom Gus had inhabited the night before.

"Goodnight my dear friends," whispered Eliza.

"Goodnight Dear," said a sleepy Jenny. "Thank you, Dear ... for everything"

"Goodnight" yawned Sebastian.

"Night" echoed Toad. Gus said nothing, he was already, apparently, the one snoring.

Eliza snuggled back under the covers and closed her eyes, listening to the sound of the rain beating against the window. She could hear the wind in the trees and was thankful her little friends were all safe and warm and tucked into bed, inside her little house. It had been quite a day, and as it was too wet and cold and dreadful outside to do any wondering, she decided maybe, for tonight, she might substitute the wondering for dreaming.

Chapter Nine

The next morning, Eliza woke to the sounds of birds chirping outside and the warmth of the sun streaming in through the window. She laid still for a moment, listening to the sounds in the house. She could hear some soft bustling she thought might be coming from the direction of the little house, so she assumed her little friends were waking up too. She could hear her mother and father talking softly in the kitchen and could smell the coffee which would undoubtedly, be perking and bubbling on the back of the stove. She could smell something else as well. Mother had made biscuits!

Eliza sat up in bed and whispered "good morning" in the direction of the little house. No sooner had she spoke, than her friends, minus Sebastian, Snip and Toad, came bustling up the comforter to the end of the bed.

"I hope we didn't wake you, Dear," said Jenny, "we've only come back in."

Rubbing her eyes, Eliza stretched and covered a yawn. "In?" she asked, "what d'ya mean in? Where have you been? What time is it?"

"Well Dear," said Jenny simply, "we've been out in the garden of course. We still have work to do, and after a vile storm like yesterday, there is even more!"

Eliza sat and pondered for a moment, blinking. Then, as she became more fully awake, she began to understand what Jenny was saying.

"But Jenny, however did you get out? Did anyone see you? What shall we do? Where are Sebastian and the others?" Eliza's voice was filled with concern.

Her questions tumbled out one after the other. Her little friends stood on the end of the bed, unsure of which question they should answer first.

"Don't worry Dear," said Jenny in a soothing voice, "we are quite resourceful!"

Eliza nodded and stretched again, then swung her feet to the floor.

"When the storm stopped, Sebastian and Snip went out to survey the damage. As it was such a fierce storm, there were a great number of flowers that needed bracing and some were bent so badly, they needed splints. They came back in and got the rest of us. We worked most of the night and finished as the sun was coming up."

"But however did you get out and back in again?" inquired Eliza.

"Oh, that's simple, its how we get in and out of most places… we used the emergency door."

Eliza looked confused. Gus took over the explanation.

"You see Eliza, it is extremely easy for us gnomes to end up … well, sort of ….trapped in places. We often sneak in through open doors and windows, into sheds, basements, even houses sometimes, when we need to find things to help us do our work. Bit's of string, some scraps of rags for bandages even occasionally, odds and ends that are not important to anybody else but are quite important to us. When we do, it is often the door, or window or whatever gets closed locking us in. We can only use our emergency doors to get us out of places. We can not use them to get us into places." Jenny nodded in agreement.

"So, Sebastian used his emergency door, to get to the other side of your little window over there, that is closest to the tree. Then, with him and Snip on one side and the three of us on the other, we were able to get the window open enough we could pass in and out without notice. Sebastian then went to work, and with Snip's help, rigged up a zip line to get us down into the garden quickly. We could then climb the tree to get back up."

It all sounded rather simple the way Gus said it, but Eliza knew how tall the tree was and how difficult it was to climb as she had attempted many times, and hadn't gotten any further than the big fork, slightly above her head.

"I am afraid," said Jenny sadly, "we have some dreadfully bad news. We had come back in so we could tell you."

This startled Eliza and she looked to her friends genuinely concerned.

"What's happened?" she asked.

"Well, it seems, Mr. Ulmus has had a rather bad time of it." Said Jenny sorrowfully. "He has had a limb badly broken and I am not sure we will be able to be of much assistance. He definitely will not be in the mood to be approached now."

"Oh dear!" exclaimed Eliza. "I must get dressed at once and then we shall all go out and take a look."

Eliza began to scurry about her room, finding shorts, a shirt, and sandals for her feet. She quickly ran a brush through her hair and slipped on a headband to keep it out of her eyes. Mother would finish fixing it once she was down at the table, but to tell the truth, she was far more worried about Mr. Ulmus than she was breakfast. Her little friends, however, would need to eat as well.

"I shall go down for breakfast immediately," she stated, "then I shall bring you all something to eat and we shall then come up with a plan."

"Don't worry about us Dear," said Jenny patiently, "We have all eaten ages ago. You get your breakfast, and we will meet you outside in your shed when you are done."

She watched as her little friends trundled across her bed, then over the nightstand and across the dresser to the windowsill. Gus jumped up first, then lending a hand to Jenny, helped her to safety as well. They both gave a bit of a wave, then nimbly scooted under the window and disappeared down the zipline. It all happened so quickly Eliza could barely see them. She was beginning to understand why she had never seen her friends in the garden before. Their clothes blended in so perfectly with all the greens and browns in the garden and they moved so quickly, one could easily mistake them for a hummingbird.

Eliza ran down the stairs and whirled into the dining room in a flourish.

"Good Morning Eliza," said her Father. "You look ready to face the day." She gave Father a big hug and then ran over to give Mother a good morning kiss. Then she shimmied up onto her chair. Mother had in fact been making biscuits this morning and Eliza was delighted to see there was already one split open, spread with raspberry jam, cooling on her plate. While she ate, Mother recombed her hair and put in her customary pigtails, then sat down to finish her tea.

It wasn't until she heard her father discussing the storm, she started to pay attention to what they were saying. Father had also been out in the garden to see what damage the storm had done, and apparently, there had been quite a bit. He and Mother were discussing what was to be done first. Mother was going to go out and tend to the garden to stake the tomato plants and gather up all the bits that had been broken off.

Father was first to rake the path, then needed to right the rain barrels and deal with the broken back gate. Eliza was paying attention without trying to be too obvious as normally, these types of grown-up things were not particularly interesting. Then her father said something that definitely caught her attention.

"I think," he said, with concern in his voice, "I will have to talk to Mr. McGuigan and get his opinion on what should be done about the elm tree."

"What has happened to the tree, Father?" asked Eliza.

"Well my girl, the storm last night was quite bad, and I am afraid the poor old tree took a bad beating. It has several broken limbs and one that is awfully bad indeed. I am afraid we may have to cut down the whole tree, but Mr. McGuigan will know the best course of action, I think. Once I have the rest of the garden put to rights, he and I will talk it over."

Oh, this was awfully bad news indeed. Eliza quickly finished her milk then asked to be excused and cleared her plate and glass without Mother having to remind her.

Eliza hurried out of the house and down the garden path and into her shed. Her friends were all waiting for her and she could see Mr. McGuigan on his garden stool, sitting on the other side of the two-way door.

"Whatever are we to do?" panted Eliza, out of breath.

"Well," said Mr. McGuigan, "I have taken a quick look and I think what we have here, is an excellent opportunity for negotiation."

Her little friends all nodded in agreement.

Eliza looked at him in confusion.

"But Father said the tree may have to come down!" she exclaimed, definitely more agitated than the others seemed to be.

Mr. McGuigan shook his head.

"No Eliza. I do not think so, however, it does need a great deal of repair. Some of it will take a lot of work and time. Your friends here though, can make that time a great deal shorter and it gives us the chance, you see, to talk to Mr. Ulmus about the door."

Eliza was confused. How on earth did the fact that the elm tree, having so many broken branches and damage, help them in talking with him about the door. She could not figure out the connection.

"You see Dear," said Jenny, rushing toward her. "We can help Mr. Ulmus heal his branches, and therefore, we can ask him if in return, to repay us, he will allow us to lean our door against him".

Jenny was speaking so quickly, and the other little men were chattering so loudly with Mr. McGuigan, it was hard for Eliza to hear her. Eliza sat for a moment trying to take in all the new information. Finally, the others all stopped talking as if they were waiting for her to reply. She looked at Mr. McGuigan and the others and they all nodded their agreement.

Eliza stopped and thought for a moment, then, blinked and sat up straight.

"So, you mean if you are somehow able to help Mr. Ulmus, then he may want to help you, to say thank you?"

"Precisely," said Gus, matter of fact-ly.

Eliza was much more excited now. It certainly did change things. How could a grumpy old tree, who now needed the gnome's help, say no after receiving their kind help to heal him? It all did make the most logical sense.

Gus, Snip, and Sebastian were then dispatched to go and have a word with Mr. Ulmus. They knew he must be feeling positively wretched and must be in the most excruciating pain, so knew they must act quickly.

Jenny and Toad were left in charge of collecting all the special plants they would need to help heal Mr. Ulmus as they were quite certain, in such a circumstance as this, there positively wasn't any way for him to say no.

Jenny explained to Eliza how many of the plants which grow in the garden had wonderful, special abilities to heal things. Meanwhile, Toad scurried about collecting roots, leaves, and even flowers. Many of the plants could be used as medicine and for someone like a tree, it was always the best way to go. Knowing what parts of what plants to use and what plants to use together was a special talent of garden gnomes and it was not too long before Toad had collected an impressive pile of all sorts of different plant material.

Jenny then set to work chopping and mashing and rubbing different plant bits and pieces together to make different potions. When Toad came back, with what looked to Eliza as a very nasty bunch of nettles, Jenny explained that even though the nettles would sting, they could also be used for the tree to diminish the pain he must be feeling.

Mr. McGuigan was dispatched to help her Father, and to keep him as far away from the tree as possible. Eliza was sent back into the garden, to pick up as many bits and pieces of twigs and branches which belonged to Mr. Ulmus as she could find. This would be the wood they would use for the door. She was also particularly instructed to make sure to pick up any pieces of bark she found, as it would be absolutely the best thing, they could use to help Mr. Ulmus heal. Bark was also very decorative and would help to make a beautiful door if they could find more than what they needed for the medicine.

The friends all went to work, and the little shed became a flurry of activity as they prepared everything they would need. Eliza was able to fill a rather large box with twigs and small branches, acorns, and a surprising amount of bark she gathered from the area beneath the poor old tree. She even, at one point, because she really wasn't sure what else to do as the old tree really must have been feeling quite dreadful, wrapped her small arms as far as she could around the trunk, and gave him a hug.

"I am so very sorry, Mr. Ulmus," she said, her voice a bit shaky. "Don't worry, help is on the way. You will feel better soon." Eliza was quite sure she heard a rather loud sniff.

Eliza could hear Mr. McGuigan and her father approaching the poor old tree.

"Perhaps," said her father "it would be best to chop down the poor old boy."

Eliza was certain, she felt the tree shudder.

"Oh no Father!" she exclaimed, "we mustn't do that! There must be a way to help him. Please Father, please help to fix him!"

Her father looked at Eliza standing with her arms about the giant tree trunk. Then he and Mr. McGuigan took a few steps back and spent a great deal of time pointing and talking and occasionally nodding or shaking their heads. Finally, it appeared, that they made a decision. Her father went scurrying into his workshop and Eliza could hear much hammering and sawing and banging about.

Mr. McGuigan had done likewise and was soon back with a number of lengths of rope and some long strips of cloth for bandages. Her father emerged from the workshop with several odd-looking boards, hammered together at different lengths. Mr. McGuigan and Father then set to work, bracing limbs of the old tree which needed support, tying others together and doing what they could to repair as much of the damage as possible.

Once they had done all they could, Mr. McGuigan suggested perhaps they should go in for tea, and then they could perhaps, decide what else could be done if Father could look up some suggestions from one of his gardening books.

Mr. McGuigan then looked very pointedly at Eliza.

"And you, young lady, you stay here and hug this old tree and let him know he is going to be fine. It is very important he not be left alone now. Do you think you can do that?" Mr. McGuigan gave Eliza a wink, then glanced pointedly toward the shed and then up into the branches of the tree, then winked at her again. Eliza nodded.

"Oh yes Mr. McGuigan, I can certainly do that! Poor old tree."

Mr. McGuigan grinned and ruffled the top of her head. "Good girl." He said, then turned her father toward the house.

Once the gentlemen had gone into the house, Eliza immediately heard her friends bustling about under the bushes toward the big tree. She had barely sat down at its base when Sebastian and Snip appeared out of nowhere.

"All set!" they exclaimed. "He's ready when we are. Let's get to work."

Sebastian bounded back up into the tree, pulling a vine behind him. He pulled the vine over one of the branches not damaged by the storm, and then as quickly, bounded back down. Eliza watched in fascination as Jenny, her arms full of stiff feathers, walked straight up the side of the tree, followed by Toad, his arms full of the squiggly bits that hold the sweet pea flowers onto their supports.

They dropped their load on a wide branch and then called down, expectantly. Eliza could only watch in wonder as the little people went to work. The vine carried bundles of materials up to the branch where Toad unloaded them. Soon, there were ever so many bundles, that Toad needed to move to another branch. Eliza was quite amazed at how nimble Toad was, especially as he was such a roly-poly little fellow.

Once that was done, and everything was where it needed to be. Sebastian, Snip, and Gus joined the others. Sebastian being much younger and far more agile, simply bounded up the tree. The others walked. Eliza could hear Jenny's soft voice, gently soothing the old tree. She was still hugging the old elm tree and was certain she could feel him occasionally shudder. Poor old tree.

The friends went to work, applying the different potions Jenny had made, stitching together the frayed wood as well as bandaging and splinting the broken branches too small for her Father and Mr. McGuigan to worry about. It was quite amazing how, when they applied the different potions, and bandages, the tree seemed to immediately be healed. Some of the more severe damage, needed to have the nettles applied first and Eliza could almost feel the tree brace itself for the sting, but then immediately relax and allow the gnomes to do their work.

The little friends scurried from branch to branch, applying potions and bandages and before long, they had come to the big branches with the most damage that Father and Mr. McGuigan had braced. The little folk took their time, standing and discussing the best way to go about helping the poor old tree. It appeared, from what Eliza could understand, the bracing her Father had used, was in fact, most suitable, which made her extremely happy. Still, it seemed, the gnomes were most concerned even with their care, the damage might, be too great.

"Do you think you might be able to mend it?" Eliza said hopefully.

"I don't know Dear," said Jenny, "we will try our best, but the damage is bad indeed. We won't know for sure until the morning."

Eliza nodded sadly, she knew her friends cared deeply for the old tree and were doing their best. She watched intently, as the little gnomes packed, and bound and knitted what bits of torn wood together they could. They packed the branch with potions and some of the bundles of leaves they had hauled up into the tree and then bound it with bandages. It was quite a wonder to Eliza how, when she looked back at some of the other branches they had bandaged, she could not make out the bandages at all. She knew they were there, but they were nearly impossible to see and if she had not known they were there, she would never have been able to pick them out.

Before too long, her friends were making their way back down the tree. Gus was sadly shaking his head and all the little folk seemed genuinely concerned.

"That's a bad one, Miss Eliza," said Gus, his concern evident in his voice. "I don't know, don't know."

All of her little friends were saddened by the severity of the damage.

It was a sad little group that retired to Eliza's shed. Everyone was deep in thought, concerned for the old tree and his severely damaged branches, the one most particularly.

"Eliza?" Mr. McGuigan said from right outside the shed, on his side of the garden, "are the wee folk with you?"

"Yes Mr. McGuigan, we are all here."

"Would you be wantin' to come to the workshop? We have some work to do."

"OH YES! Please, may we?" Eliza said excitedly. Her little friends had brightened considerably at the sound of the old man's voice. The reminder there was still a door to build, seemed to cheer everyone up and the group jumped to their feet and began to talk excitedly.

"Make sure you bring all the bits my girl" Mr. McGuigan reminded her.

Eliza gathered together all the bits of twig, wood pieces and bark she had gathered from the garden. Jenny and the others, after asking permission from Eliza, had searched through her treasures finding some shells, acorns and a few brightly coloured stones, which they thought would add considerably to the beauty of the new door. They then, quickly, but carefully, watching out for Mr. Jones, made their way to Mr. McGuigan's workshop.

Chapter Ten

Once inside the workshop, Eliza and her friends carefully laid out all the materials so Mr. McGuigan could have a look. It did seem like there was quite a bit of wood, but all the pieces were quite small. It was hard to tell if there would be enough to make a fine door to lean against the old tree. Mr. McGuigan stood back looking at the bits and pieces laid out on his workbench and scratched his mostly bald head.

"Well?" queried Gus "do we have enough?"

"There is plenty here for the frame and for the door jam and the like, but I am afraid we don't have any pieces large enough to make the actual door out of. We could piece a number of the small bits together, but I would have to use glue and that won't do, as it is completely man-made, so then, even if we did get enough together to make the door, it wouldn't work anyway."

The little folk all nodded in agreement.

"Let's get out a bit of paper and see what we can come up with for the rest. Then perhaps, we will be able to find a solution" suggested Mr. McGuigan. Eliza searched the shelf nearest her and managed to come up with a few sheets of dusty paper and a half of a broken pencil. Mr. McGuigan set to work, listening intently to the instructions of the gnomes and began drawing what appeared to Eliza to be the most magnificent door she had seen. It was certainly more spectacular than any they had seen in the book and she could see her friends becoming more and more excited.

They worked through the morning until Eliza's mother called from the garden it was time for her to come in for lunch. Promising lunch to her friends as well, Eliza hurried home.

When she was finished, Eliza once again skipped down the garden path towards her little shed. The wind had come up a bit and she had paused a moment by the old tree to give him a reassuring hug. She was quite concerned with the wind, as when it gusted around the garden, it made the brace Father had put under the badly broken branch, sway alarmingly. She had barely made it into the workshop to tell Mr. McGuigan when a loud crack pierced the air.

Eliza, Mr. McGuigan, and their friends all ran out into the garden to see what had happened. Her father had appeared out of his workshop as well. It was as Eliza had feared. The wind had come up and gusted through the garden a bit too hard. It had wobbled the brace from under the big branch. The brace had fallen to the ground, and with nothing to support it, the big branch had torn away even more and was now hanging half attached and half not, down onto the ground.

Mr. McGuigan hugged Eliza to him to comfort her, as tears slid down her cheeks. Poor old tree.

"Well then, that's ghastly," said Father. Gus tapped Eliza's foot.

"Miss Eliza, Miss Eliza!!" he said urgently. You must get your Father to saw the branch off cleanly. It must come off now and there is simply no other way to do it. It must be a clean-cut, next to the trunk to remove all the damaged wood. He must do it right away!"

Mr. McGuigan heard their little friend and waving his hand, called out to her father.

"Let me give you a hand Thomas, I have the saw to fix that right up." Eliza's father waved back, accepting the help. They all bustled back into Mr. McGuigan's workshop.

"Tell me, friends," he said to the group. "Tell me exactly what and how I need to take the branch off to save that old tree and cause as little damage as possible."

Jenny and Toad, being as it appeared to be the experts on trees, gave Mr. McGuigan very precise instructions on the type of saw to use, and how to sever the branch correctly. Mr. McGuigan listened very carefully.

"Once you are done," said Jenny, "come back and I will have a potion ready you can spread on the wound to help it heal. I will have to make a large batch and it will take some time."

She immediately turned and gave the rest of the group their instructions. Eliza could tell by how everyone listened and did as they were told with no argument, the situation was serious.

"What may I do Jenny, please, is there a task for me?" Eliza wanted to help, and at 6 and ¾ and 4 days old, she was sure there must be something she could do.

"Yes Dear, of course, we need your help!" Jenny seemed surprised that Eliza thought there was any chance she might not!

"Run to your little shed and try to find anything that might do for a bowl, it needs to be rather large if you can manage it, one of your mother's soup bowls would do nicely, but I don't suppose you will have one like that."

"Oh! I do, I do!" exclaimed Eliza excitedly, "Mother chipped one last week and she said I might have it as she was going to buy new ones!"

"Excellent, that's a stroke of luck if ever there was" stated

Jenny, pleased with Eliza's news.

"Now listen very carefully. I will give you a list of things to do and you must do them in a very particular order." Eliza nodded, listening intently.

Jenny proceeded to instruct Eliza carefully. First, she was to find enough fresh, green moss as she could, to line the bowl with. She was then to pluck a couple of large Hosta leaves and lay those on top of the moss. If one would work, it would be better. Then, she needed to visit as many flowers in the garden as possible still wet with the rain from last night. She was to ask politely if she may have permission to tap or shake them gently, and if they would release what water they had, into her little bowl. Jenny told her this was a job only a child could do as flowers would never be able to understand a grown-up. Then, she must find as many Peony petals which had fallen onto the ground, as it took to completely cover the water in the bowl.

"But if it's rainwater you need Jenny, why can't we take it from the barrel at the bottom of the eaves?"

"Because Dear," said Jenny gently, "the eaves and the barrel have all been made, this rainwater must have never touched anything not from the natural world. By lining your bowl with moss and then with a large leaf, we can keep it from touching the bowl itself. It is the only way, Dear. We can't get any of our tools, so we are going to have to make do".

Jenny had told her quite seriously, if any of the flowers seemed too standoffish, Eliza should tell them she had sent her.

Eliza nodded and scampered down the pathway and into her shed. It did not take her long to locate the bowl and she was soon out in the garden hunting for moss. She managed to find the type Jenny had asked for, right along the fence between her garden and the McGuigan's, under the shade of the elm tree. She carefully picked some and gently laid it in her bowl, pushing it up along the sides and adding bits here and there until the bowl was completely covered.

Her next task was to find a big enough Hosta leaf to completely fill the inside of the bowl. Eliza remembered the first night, next to the garden steps and the Hosta she had found Gus hiding under. She ran to the step, being careful not to jostle the moss in the bowl and sat down beside the garden on the bottom-most step, next to the little handprint and the shiny blue stone.

"Mr. Hosta, might you have a leaf that I can use for the gnomes? The elm tree is very damaged and in need of some surgery and Jenny sent me to gather some water."

Eliza was quite amazed when, as she sat quite still, her little bowl in her hands resting on the ground, a Hosta leaf seemed to drop out of nowhere and fill her little bowl perfectly. She then saw a few drops of water, spill down another leaf and into her bowl. One after another, the broad leaves seemed to nod toward her, rivulets of water trickled down, one leaf to the next, and into her bowl. In a moment, there was quite a little puddle in the bottom of her bowl.

Thanking the Hosta plant profusely, Eliza quickly went on with her work. Running here and there, politely asking the flowers for water and mentioning she was on an errand for Jenny. The flowers all gave what water they had, and it was not long before the little bowl was as full as Eliza dared carry. She found the huge, round, pink blossoms of the Peony bush and again, asking sweetly, and repeating her errand, was quite thrilled to see one of the huge flowers, release a few petals which dropped elegantly down onto the surface of the water in her bowl, without her even having to touch them. Her errand completed, Eliza moved slowly and carefully, back to the shed, careful, not to spill even one drop.

Jenny was bustling back and forth on the workbench on which was placed a rather large, wooden bowl. It was the type her mother used to make salad.

"Isn't it wonderful" beamed Jenny. "Your friend Mr. McGuigan brought it to us. I have no idea where he found it, but it is a perfect size and it's made of wood!"

Jenny was clearly pleased and as Eliza watched, began adding berries, leaves and what Toad declared to be pollen, into the bottom of the big, round, wooden bowl. Sebastian was in the bowl and was stomping his feet, mashing all the ingredients together. Eliza giggled, he looked like the pictures she had seen of people stomping grapes to get the juice out.

Once they were satisfied, Jenny asked Eliza to carefully pour the water, little by little, into the bowl. Jenny stirred the ingredients together with a long twig as if she were making a cake. Occasionally, she would ask the others for a bit of this or that or would ask Eliza for a bit more water. Finally, she was satisfied. Eliza thought the entire workshop smelled like chamomile, lavender, and roses, which would only make sense, as chamomile tea was what Mother gave her when she was not feeling well. Eliza hoped it would help Mr. Ulmus feel better too.

The little group waited until Mr. McGuigan came through the door, huffing, and puffing. Everyone looked at him, expectantly, as he sat down on his stool to catch his breath.

"All done," he said. "Poor old tree, but I think he will be fine. It did leave quite a gaping hole in the canopy though. There is quite a lot more sunshine in the garden with the branch gone." The others nodded sadly.

"Well then, about the potion". Jenny explained to Mr. McGuigan the importance of not touching the potion with his hands and how he must use a large leaf or piece of bark to spread it on the wound. Mr. McGuigan listened carefully, and after a bit of a rest, went out with a ladder so he might more easily reach where he needed, and returned for the wooden basin full of the potion. In his hand, was a couple of exceptionally large rhubarb leaves he then folded into a neat packet that Jenny, nodding in approval, felt would be a good tool to apply the potion.

"I would invite you all to come with," he said, then whispered "but Mr. Jones is about, and we can't have any more excitement today. It is too fine a day for Mrs. M. to be keeping him in the house. You will be safe in here, don't be venturing out without Eliza to protect you."

Gus blustered at Mr. McGuigan's warning. Fool cat! They had many run-ins, with the fat, old cat and he had not won yet! Still, today had been upsetting enough and the thought of his new friends having to rescue him again, or any of the others, after having been so helpful with dealing with the tree, thought it would be wisest if they all, Eliza included, remained in the workshop.

Mr. McGuigan congratulated him on his wise thinking and having rested enough, picked up the basin and his packet of rhubarb leaves, and went out to apply the potion to Mr. Ulmus. In no time at all, he was back, the basin wiped clean as Mr. McGuigan had taken great care to use every bit of the potion Jenny had made, to cover the saw wound left after he had cut off the broken limb.

"Well then," he said, "that's a right tidy job if I do say so myself."

The little group was all sitting on the workbench, they were not as jovial today as it had been quite a difficult day and they were still all incredibly sad for the ordeal the old tree had been through.

"Now then," he said, "don't be looking so glum! There was nothing else could be done and the old tree, despite having a branch removed, I dare say, is none the worse for wear... and...I have something else, also!"

Mr. McGuigan stepped back out of the shop and then reappeared, holding a large chunk of the branch he had removed from the tree.

"Would you be thinking," he said, his eyes sparkling a bit "we might be able to make a door out of this?"

The little folk looked at each other as if in shock. Then they all began to laugh and chatter at the same time. Snip and Sebastian linked arms and began to dance around. Gus grabbed up Jenny in a hug then twirled her in a circle, her skirts fluttering as he did. Toad, well Toad was doing his absolute best rendition of a jig, of course until he became quite out of breath and sat down with a plop, puffing. Eliza ran over to Mr. McGuigan and hugged him tightly.

"However, did you manage it?" she asked excitedly.

Mr. McGuigan sat the big chunk of tree branch on the end of the workbench with a thump and sat down on his stool, wiping his forehead with his handkerchief.

"Well," he stated simply, "once the branch was off, I didn't think we would be needin' permission from the old tree. So, I lopped off one end of it to see if we could make something out of it."

Gus bustled over and patted his friend's arm. Toad waddled over to shake Mr. McGuigan's finger and Sebastian and Snip shook each other's hands. Jenny tugged on Eliza's sleeve and Eliza lifted her up so that she could bestow a kiss on Mr.

McGuigan's cheek. Gus was not amused.

They were about to start back to work on the drawings for the door, when Mrs. McGuigan knocked on the door and then, opening the top half of the door, called to Eliza that her mother was calling her in for dinner.

Eliza answered she would be up directly, and Mrs. McGuigan shut the door. Mr. McGuigan had a few more questions for their friends, so they, still having a great deal of work to do in the garden, told her not to worry about them and to go in and have her supper. Tonight, would be bath time again and Eliza was quite sure, it would take ever so long. Sebastian put her mind to rest.

"Don't be frettin' Miss Eliza. That zip line is far easier for us to move about without notice, than being bounced about in your little crate, as much as we appreciated the rescue. No. We will be fine, and we will meet you up in your room before dark. We can make ourselves quite invisible you know, but it would be very much appreciated if, at some point, you were able to find us a bit of something to eat."

Nodding that she would, Eliza gave Mr. McGuigan an extra big hug for all his help with the tree, for everything he had done for her little friends and because, well, he was so frightfully special.

Much, much later…Eliza had finished her bath, had her story, and had even had some playtime with her father and was sitting down to her snack when her friends made their appearance on her windowsill. She had asked Mother for a rather large snack and so was busily sharing her crackers, cheese, pickles, and a good helping of berries from the garden, into gnome size helpings. She even had a couple of leftover cookies from dinner that she had pilfered after she had cleared her plate. All in all, it was a rather nice dinner for her friends, as she was sure they must be very hungry.

The gnomes had worked extremely hard all day, putting everything to right again, out in the garden. There had been a couple of wee birds, who could not yet fly, who needed help to get back into their nest. The ladybugs and June bugs were scattered hither and yon and had to be rounded up again. There were ever so many broken flowers to be splinted and some rather difficult slugs, who thought they might make their way onto Father's prize roses, that needed to be persuaded otherwise.

Eliza listened intently, she was learning ever so much and would never again, take a rainstorm for granted. She did, however, like to watch the lightning and listen to the thunder roll, but she would now have a much greater appreciation for how much work it could be for her little friends when such a storm rolled through town.

It was not long before all the goodies Mother had brought her for her snack had been eaten. It had been an exceptionally long day and her little friends were all very tired, and very dirty. Eliza went to the bathroom and brought back two rather large glasses of hot, soapy water so that her friends might each have fresh clean water to bathe in. She carefully laid out some of the bits of an old towel that she had found that her mother said she might have, although why Eliza would want an old rag had clearly been a mystery to her.

Once everything was in place, and her friends were tucked away nicely into the little house, she called her mother for her tuck in. Eliza snuggled right down and was nearly fast asleep when Father came in. He simply tucked her in a bit more and kissed her on the top of her head. Then turning, he flicked out the light, although he was quite sure he heard water splashing in Eliza's little dollhouse, he shook his head and wondered if it was his imagination.

Chapter Eleven

Morning came with birds chirping, the warm sun streaming through the window, and Gus, persistently pulling on Eliza's hair.

"Wake up! Wake up!" he shouted insistently. Eliza heard Jenny admonish him gently.

"Be gentle Dear, gen....tle"

Eliza opened one eye and peered, blurr-idly at her dear little friends, then grinning impishly at Gus, answered his request with a sleepy, "Why?"

Gus looked at her for a moment, as if trying to comprehend what she had said.

"FRUMPDUMPLINGS" he hollered. Jenny shushed him.

"Diggermuffins!" he continued to exclaim "there's work to do!!"

Eliza chuckled. "Of course, Gus. I was teasing."

Shuffling to get out from under her covers, Eliza swung her feet to the floor, almost hitting Toad in the process. Toad jumped out of the way, and after a quick apology to her little friend, Eliza made her bed and proceeded to get her clothes picked out. Jenny shoed the menfolk out of Eliza's room and she quickly dressed.

"Now Dear," said Jenny. "If you wouldn't mind hurrying a little bit, Mr. McGuigan is waiting for us."

"Of course, Jenny," said Eliza, feeling bad she had kept them all waiting. "I will meet you at Mr. McGuigan's. Have you all eaten?"

"Oh yes, Mr. McGuigan had the loveliest bowl of porridge for us. It has been such a long time since I have had a really, lovely bowl of porridge." Jenny said wistfully. "We have all eaten Dear and as it is quite late… do hurry Dear."

Jenny popped up onto the bed, then onto the bedside table, and then the windowsill. She blew Eliza a kiss as she scooted under the window and disappeared.

Eliza ran down the stairs and whirled into the dining room, quickly sitting down on her chair, and reaching for the piece of toast her mother offered her.

"And what are you going to be up to today young lady? I have hardly seen anything of you all week and your mother says you have been very occupied over at Mr. McGuigan's. Do be careful that you aren't making a nuisance of yourself my dear." Father admonished her gently.

"Oh no, Father."

Suddenly, the phone rang. Father got up to answer it and was smiling at Eliza as he said "No, Mrs. McGuigan, she's here, finishing her breakfast. She seems to be running a bit late."

Father said goodbye and hung up the phone.

"Well Eliza, that was Mrs. McGuigan and apparently, whatever you and Mr. McGuigan have been up to in that workshop of his cannot continue without you, and Mrs. McGuigan called to hurry you along."

Father winked at Mother, who was already spreading another piece of toast with peanut butter and placing it on top of the slice she held with jam.

"There you go young lady, PB&J, a most adequate breakfast.

Now run along, you mustn't keep Mr. McGuigan waiting." Her mother handed her the sandwich and Eliza jumped down from her chair and kissed her mother on the cheek. She was almost out the door when her father called her back.

"Pray, tell me Eliza?" he asked, "whatever are you working on out there?"

"Oh, nothing Father, we are making a gnome door!" and with that, Eliza was out the door and down the steps heading to her shed. She was halfway to the shed before she realized what she had said. Oh well, too late now! Father would not have believed her anyway. He did not believe in fairy stories.

Out in the workshop, there was a great deal of commotion. Mr. McGuigan had in fact, been working extremely hard on the door, and had surprised the gnomes with a door beyond comparison.

They had all gathered, after their chores, in the workshop to wait for Eliza to get up. Mr. McGuigan had worked late in the night and had been at it again very early this morning and when the gnomes saw his light on, decided to see what he was up to, while they waited on their dear little friend.

Mr. McGuigan was delighted to see them and surprised them with the door he was finishing working on. Gus had been overwhelmed by the amount of attention Mr. McGuigan had paid to constructing the door. It was sound and sturdy and had bits of leather for hinges.

The door was cut from the large piece of branch which had fallen from the tree. He had deliberately sliced the branch on the diagonal which made the slab much larger and an interesting oval shape. One end had been cut off, so it was straight and flat for the bottom. Then, he had sanded the wood very carefully, and rubbed it with bee's wax to make is shine and also protect it from the rain. The door had then been mounted in a frame, to allow it to open, with the frame remaining in contact with the tree it was leaned up against. All along the frame of the door were beautiful carvings of flowers and creatures from the garden. They were so tiny but perfectly carved that even Gus was impressed beyond measure.

Mr. McGuigan was a skilled woodsman and had worked hard on the door and the gnomes were deeply touched. Now, they were extremely excited to share it with Eliza, as she was the one who had brought them all together in the first place. Mr. McGuigan heard Eliza skipping up the path and quickly covered the door with a cloth.

Eliza knocked, then opening the bottom of the door stepped into the workshop. All her friends were standing on one side of the workbench and Mr. McGuigan was behind it. They all seemed excited. Gus could barely stand still.

"What took you so long!" he exclaimed.

"Gus be polite" Jenny scolded. Gus apologized. "I'm sorry, it's that we have been waiting so long!"

"It's all right Jenny," Eliza said, then turned to Gus. "I am deeply sorry Gus. I did not mean to sleep so late. Now, what is all the fuss about?"

The little friends asked her to close her eyes, then Mr. McGuigan led her over to the workbench and picked her up to sit on the very end. Only then, was she allowed to open her eyes. All Eliza could see, was a large… something, under a cloth. She looked up at Mr. McGuigan questioningly.

Mr. McGuigan grinned, then turned to Gus.

"All right then, wee Gus.

You can do the honours!"

With all the might he could muster, and a great deal of flourish too, Gus whipped the cloth from the door. Sebastian was sitting on the light over the workbench and leaned back a bit so that the light was directed right at the door.

"Oohhhhhh" said Eliza, in a hushed voice. "Mr. McGuigan! It's the most beautiful thing I have ever seen!"

Eliza reached out to caress the carvings lovingly. Mr. McGuigan had even captured each of their little friends in the carvings and she could not have thought of anything more perfect.

The friends all sat together, admiring the many details on the beautiful door. It was finally Toad, who brought them back to the task at hand.

"B...b....b...but we haven't g....g....gotten him to s....s.... say yes!"

Everyone stopped.

Then, everyone started talking all at once! Finally, Sebastian, letting out a shrill whistle, got everyone to stop once again.

"Goodness!" exclaimed Jenny. "We completely forgot!"

"Saints preserve us!" said Mr. McGuigan sitting down hard, on his stool.

All the friends could do was to keep looking back and forth at one another, wondering what to do, until finally, Eliza spoke up.

"Mr. McGuigan can you please lift me down?" This was the first thing at hand as she was still sitting on top of the workbench.

"Let us go, Jenny! The rest of you may come along if you wish."

Mr. McGuigan lifted Sebastian down off the light, his bounding about was hard on Mr. McGuigan's nerves. Then he lifted all the wee folk off the workbench. He covered the door again with the cloth and they all set out for Eliza's garden. Eliza and the gnomes went through her shed, and Mr. McGuigan through the back-garden gate, meeting as a group, around the base of the old elm tree.

Jenny approached the tree first.

"Cara maith daor maidin, ni thiocfaidh tu` amach"

She said lovingly, as she caressed the old tree. Gus explained to Eliza that it meant "good morning, dear friend, won't you come out", but was spoken in Gaelic.

"Gaelic? I thought you were Scandinavian?" said Eliza, a bit confused.

"Yes, we are." Said Gus, "but the flowers and trees all speak Gaelic, as it is a very old language."

Eliza nodded and watched. She saw the old tree shake ever so slightly, and then, before her eyes, appeared the face of an incredibly old, incredibly sad, gentleman. Eliza was astounded and Mr. McGuigan began rubbing his eyes under his glasses.

"There you are, dear friend," said Jenny gently. "Are you feeling any better?"

Mr. Ulmus

If it was possible, the old tree looked even sadder. Eliza could stand it no more, and moving slowly, and carefully, she edged closer to the back of the old tree and wrapped her small arms gently around him, hugging him.

The old tree sniffed.

"Is it you, dear one?" he whispered gruffly.

Eliza crept forward so that she was facing the tree.

112

"Hello, Mr. Ulmus" she whispered, in a soft small voice. "I am sorry if I disturbed you. I was hoping to make you feel a bit better."

"My child. You and your little friends here have made an old tree feel much better. Your tender care, especially your hugs, it has been a very long time since I have been hugged you know, and the help of these wee folk, as well as you Sir" directing his remark to Mr. McGuigan, "have saved this old tree. Thank you, all, for your kindness."

Mr. McGuigan nodded towards the old tree. The old gentleman was quite touched by his words.

Jenny continued, "Is there anything you need, dear friend?"

Mr. Ulmus simply rustled his leaves.

"No, nothing. You have done everything and more. It will take time to mend now."

"Oh, Mr. Ulmus! I am so deeply sorry the storm was so bad, and you were so damaged!" exclaimed Eliza. "It was dreadful we had to take off your lovely branch. I hope you can forgive us!"

"Hush child," said the old tree. "Nothing was done that wasn't necessary. It is the problem with being a tree when things like this happen, you are powerless to do anything to help yourself. You must rely on the help of others. I am truly fortunate indeed."

"Fiddlesticks," said Jenny, smiling and gently patting the grizzled cheek. "now enough about that. You will mend quite nicely, I think."

The leaves in the tree rustled.

Mr. McGuigan gave Eliza a gentle nudge and looking down at the cloth-covered door in his hands, then gave Eliza a quick wink.

Mr. Ulmus noticed it too.

"What have you there, child? What is it?" Mr. Ulmus's voice

was soft and low.

"Well you see, Mr. Ulmus," she began, "several days ago, my father installed a new back garden stair." Mr. Ulmus appeared to agree. "Well," she continued, "my friend's door to their home…was in the old stair. That is how it came to be we all became friends. Mr. McGuigan and I have been helping them build a new door."

Mr. McGuigan stepped forward and Eliza pulled the cloth from over the door so he might see it. Eliza quickly continued.

"After the storm, I gathered all the bits and pieces together, and Mr. McGuigan did such a lot of hard work and made this beautiful door from your wood… and we were wondering," Eliza paused, trying to gather her courage, "if you would allow us, my friends and I, to lay this beautiful door made of all your beautiful wood, against you, so that they may have a way to get home."

The little people shuffled a bit closer. Mr. Ulmus seemed to take a considerable length of time to make his decision.

"You mean, you came out after the storm, and collected all this? And you Sir, you put it all together and did all this beautiful work? And you want to lean it against me so these, little folk, who have worked so awfully hard to help me, might have a door to go home?"

Eliza and the rest of the group nodded, then waited patiently. Some were more patient than others, however. Gus was beginning to bluster, and Jenny shushed him gently. Now was definitely not the time for Gus to go off on one of his blusters, not now, not when Mr. Ulmus was considering their request.

Finally, the old tree began to quiver.

"Dear friends," he said, his voice quiet and low, "I can never repay you for your help and your kindness. I know I have been quite gruff before, but it has never stopped you from coming to my aid. You have mended these old branches and sticks so many times, and I have never even said thank you. Now you come to me, after doing ever so much to help me once again, and ask me if you may lay this beautiful piece of craftsmanship, made of all my own wood, against me? What else can I do? Of course, you may. It would be an honour to have your door against me. That way, I can perhaps care for you by providing some shelter, the way you have cared so diligently for me."

The little group paused for a moment, as they let his gentle words soak in. Then, they all erupted in cheers and Eliza could see the old tree smile. Mr. McGuigan stepped forward and gently settled the door into place, making very sure that it was as snug a fit as could possibly be. Once completed, Mr. McGuigan stepped back as the rest of the little group moved forward. Eliza had jumped up and once again, had wrapped her little arms around the big tree and was hugging him tightly.

Gus, Jenny, Toad, Snip, and Sebastian all gathered around the door, linking arms together and began to hum. The tune was unlike anything Eliza had heard before but was wonderfully soft and very pretty. She let go of the tree and slipped next to Mr. McGuigan who hugged her next to him. The friends continued to hum. Gus and then Sebastian, who were standing next to the tree, reached out to lay their hands on the rough bark, creating a circle that included the tree. As they did so, they all began to rock very slightly side to side in time to the music.

Eliza blinked as she saw, starting with Jenny, who was in the middle, a very faint, sparkly light began to twinkle around them. The humming became a bit louder but was still pretty, and soft, and the sparkly light began to spread. First, it spread to each of the gentle little folk, swirling around them, even tangling in their long beards making them sparkle. Then the light began to spread down over their clothes and finally, onto the ground, spreading toward the door and to the trunk of the old tree. Eliza held her breath as she watched the light twine itself across the ground and slowly begin to climb up the tree. Sparkles seemed to shimmer and rain down over the entire group until finally, the sparkles seemed to burst out the top of the tree, like fireworks.

Jenny then looked up at the old tree, "ba mhaith linn teacht abhaile" she said gently, "we would like to go home."

There was a bright flash of light behind the door, and then ever so slowly, the door began to open. Mr. McGuigan and Eliza could only stare.

Slowly, all the sparkles and trails of light faded away. The only light came from the door which was now wide open. Eliza could see tiny torches lighting the way down a long staircase. The inside of the staircase seemed to glow with a warm, welcoming light. She blinked as tears came to her eyes, for now, she realized what all this meant. Her friends could now go home, which also meant, they would no longer be staying in her room. Oh, how she was going to miss them!

Eliza sat down on the ground, cross-legged, as close as she could get to the door. Her little friends gathered round, and she lifted Jenny and Gus up onto her legs.

"Well my friends, I guess this is goodbye," she said in a hushed, sad voice. "I am ever so happy you have a way to go home, and you have such a wonderful, beautiful door in such a wonderful, kind old tree, but I shall miss you." Eliza could not stop the tear that slipped from her eye, and slid down her cheek, followed by another.

"Oh, Fiddlesticks! My dear, dear girl" said Jenny, patting Eliza's hand "this is not goodbye, why you shall see us all the time. We are friends now and we now know you would never harm us, so we will be able to visit with you all the time! The same goes for you, Mr. McGuigan! Why goodbye? The thought never crossed our minds!"

All the little folk nodded in agreement and patted whatever part of their two larger friends they could reach.

"We know we can come into your shed, and into your room and even into Mr. McGuigan's workshop, without ever having to fear, except of course for Mr. Jones, silly, old cat!" Jenny giggled.

"You will see us all the time, and I shouldn't wonder, we might join you on the back step from time to time, for a lovely visit. Now, however, we really must go. We will have so much to do down below, and it has been a rather trying few days. We do have much work still to do."

Eliza smiled and wiped her tears. It was such wonderful news!

"Thank you, Jenny, and you too Gus… and all the rest! You have become so very dear to me! I should have missed you quite dreadfully. I wish I could go with you."

"I know Dear," said Jenny, hugging Eliza as best she could, "for a child with such a gentle and kind heart as you, anything is possible."

Gus tugged at Jenny's hand and together they hopped off Eliza's leg, the others had all gathered at the doorway, and Toad, ever the gentleman, was holding the door. One by one, the little folk said their thankyou's and with a wave, proceeded to enter the doorway and begin to make their way down the steps. When the last had entered, the door closed gently behind them.

Mr. McGuigan scooped an incredibly sad Eliza up into his arms and gave her a fierce hug.

"Now my girl," he whispered. "Wasn't that an adventure!"